5! Top Pick! "An absolutely must read! From beginning to end, it's an incredible ride."
—*Night Owl Romance*

5 Hearts! "I definitely recommend *Dangerous Highlander*, even to skeptics of paranormal romance – you just may fall in love with the MacLeods."
—*The Romance Reader*

5 Angels! Recommended Read! "*Forbidden Highlander* blew me away."
—*Fallen Angel Reviews*

5 Tombstones! "Another fantastic series that melds the paranormal with the historical life of the Scottish highlander in this arousing and exciting adventure. The men of MacLeod castle are a delicious combination of devoted brother, loyal highlander Lord and demonic God that ooze sex appeal and inspire some very erotic daydreams as they face their faults and accept their fate."
—*Bitten By Books*

4 Stars! "Grant creates a vivid picture of Britain centuries after the Celts and Druids tried to expel the Romans, deftly merging magic and history. The result is a wonderfully dark, delightfully well-written tale. Readers will eagerly await the next Dark Sword book."
—*Romantic Times BOOKreviews*

**Don't miss these other spellbinding novels by
DONNA GRANT**

Dark King Series
Dark Heat
Darkest Flame
Fire Rising
Burning Desire
Hot Blooded

Dark Warrior series
Midnight's Master
Midnight's Lover
Midnight's Seduction
Midnight's Warrior
Midnight's Kiss
Midnight's Captive
Midnight's Temptation
Midnight's Promise
Midnight's Surrender

Dark Sword series
Dangerous Highlander
Forbidden Highlander
Wicked Highlander
Untamed Highlander
Shadow Highlander
Darkest Highlander

Shield Series
A Dark Guardian
A Kind of Magic
A Dark Seduction
A Forbidden Temptation
A Warrior's Heart

DRUIDS GLEN SERIES

Highland Mist
Highland Nights
Highland Dawn
Highland Fires
Highland Magic
Dragonfyre

SISTERS OF MAGIC TRILOGY

Shadow Magic
Echoes of Magic
Dangerous Magic

Royal Chronicles Novella Series

Prince of Desire
Prince of Seduction
Prince of Love
Prince of Passion

Wicked Treasures Novella Series

Seized by Passion
Enticed by Ecstasy
Captured by Desire

And look for more anticipated novels from Donna Grant

The Craving (Rogues of Scotland)
Darkest Flame (Dark Kings)
Wild Dream – (Chiasson)
Fire Rising – (Dark Kings)

coming soon!

A DARK SEDUCTION

THE SHIELDS

DONNA GRANT

This is a work of fiction. All of the characters, organizations, and events portrayed in this novel are either products of the author's imagination or are used fictitiously.

A DARK SEDUCTION

© 2012 by DL Grant, LLC
Excerpt from *A Forbidden Temptation* copyright © 2012 by Donna Grant

Cover design © 2012 by Croco Designs

ISBN 10: 0988208431
ISBN 13: 978-0988208438

All rights reserved, including the right to reproduce or transmit this book, or a portion thereof, in any form or by any means, electronic or mechanical, without permission in writing from the author. This book may not be resold or uploaded for distribution to others. Thank you for respecting the hard work of this author.

www.DonnaGrant.com

Available in ebook and print editions

CHAPTER ONE

LeBlanc village
Westmorland County, England
Summer 1244

Eyes as sharp as a falcon's scanned the crowded village as people shuffled from place to place in an effort to accomplish their chores.

All was normal in the small, sleepy village, except for two men who stood silent and unmoving against the loud backdrop.

Cole, the taller of the two by mere inches, found his gaze returning again and again to the three-story tavern. He straightened from the blacksmith shop as his hand brushed the handle of his war axe.

"What is it?"

Cole glanced at his companion. Gabriel stood tense, poised for action with his hands relaxed by his side, ready to grasp his bow and arrow at a moment's notice.

"I'm not sure," Cole finally answered. "There's

something in the tavern."

In response, Gabriel reached behind his head and drew his hair away from his face to tie it at the nape of his neck with a string of leather.

Cole grinned. "Ready for some action?"

"I was born ready," Gabriel said and flexed his shoulders.

Just as Cole lifted his foot to step into the street, a flash of yellow caught his attention. He stared, transfixed, as a shapely leg peeked out of an upstairs window.

"Is that…?"

"Aye," Cole mumbled, unable to look away.

To his delight, more leg was exposed, and then a slender arm joined in. It was only moments later that a shapely backside also moved through the narrow window.

Gabriel leaned forward for a better look. "What do you suppose she is doing?"

Cole chuckled and crossed his arms over his chest. "I've no idea, but I'm enjoying the show."

The girl managed to extract the rest of her body from the window and hung perilously by her fingers and toes on the side of the building, her faded yellow skirts pulled up between her legs and tucked into a belt around her waist.

It gave her legs room to maneuver, but Cole wasn't sure that would be enough. It took incredible hand strength to keep a hold as she was doing. Something most women didn't have.

With her dark hair coming loose of its pins and continually getting into her eyes, Cole knew she wasn't going to make it. No matter how courageous she was in attempting such an act.

"She's going to plunge to her death."

Cole happened to agree. Yet, by the way the woman hung on, as if she didn't have a care in the world, he had a feeling she knew exactly what she was doing.

"She's not in a hurry," Cole said as he glanced at the open window to see if anyone followed her.

Gabriel snorted. "Then why in the name of the Fae is she climbing down the tavern?"

Cole shrugged and involuntarily took a step toward the woman when her foot slipped.

"We need to do something," Gabriel stated, as he looked first one way and then the other.

Cole was surprised they were the only ones who noticed the woman. She hung above the villagers, and could come crashing down atop one of them at any moment, yet no one looked her way.

A smile pulled at his lips as the woman slowly worked her way to the corner of the building and then climbed down. He heard Gabriel mumble something beneath his breath when her feet touched the ground and she untucked her skirts from betwixt her legs.

All Cole managed to see through the throng of people were strands of brunette hair that his fingers longed to plunge into. She had caught his attention as any women who would brave such dangers would.

He couldn't wait to have her in his arms.

Before he could go to her, Gabriel's hand on his arm stopped him. "There's no time."

Cole looked back toward the woman. She was just

making her escape from town when two men caught her and roughly dragged her back into the tavern.

It was just as well, Cole thought. His cock would have to wait while he and Gabriel gathered what information they could.

With his mind set to forget the woman, he took a deep breath and began to turn away. Anger sliced through him when one of the men backhanded her so hard she fell to the ground.

It took every ounce of will he had for Cole to turn away.

He couldn't make a scene, not yet.

Not until they knew what evil lurked in the small village.

It was only the defiant look the woman threw her assailants as she got to her feet that allowed him to keep a semblance of composure.

"We'll take care of those men when we get back," Gabriel said.

"Aye. I look forward to it."

Just thinking of cleaving the men in two with his axe brought a measure of calm. But it was a small measure.

Cole found his fingers gripping the handle of his axe when the woman was shoved into the tavern.

It was Gabriel's hand upon his shoulder that got his attention. "Let's go," Gabriel said.

With one last look at the woman's retreating back, Cole turned away. As they walked down the road toward the castle high up on the hill, he found Gabriel fingering his dagger. Gabriel had a keen sense that the Shields always listened to. Cole wasn't about to ignore it now.

"What is it?"

"The castle," Gabriel murmured. "There is something about it, something that doesn't seem quite...normal."

Cole's eyes immediately went to the imposing stone towers that reached toward the clouds. "You think the evil resides there?"

Gabriel shrugged and slowed his pace. "In the past, anytime the Fae have moved us through time, we always arrive once the creature has begun to plague the village."

Cole nodded, following Gabriel's line of thought. "Yet no one acts as though their lives are in danger. Do you suppose the creature hasn't yet arrived?"

"Nay, it's here. Aimery said as much."

Aimery. Cole wished the Fae commander were with them to shed more light on their quest. Being a Shield was something Cole prided himself on, but a little more information could be as valuable as gold.

Gabriel punched him on the arm. "Don't tell me you still dislike being thrown into a time and place you know nothing about."

Cole shook his head at the grin on Gabriel's face. It was a rare occurrence when Gabriel smiled, not to mention jested, and after all they had been through with being separated from Val and Roderick, then losing Darrick to death and Hugh to his heart mate, Cole could barely muster a grin, much less jest.

"Knowing what we're up against could give us an added edge, at least."

This time Gabriel chuckled. "As if you need it. An

immortal who can wield a war axe like others use a sword."

It was true, but Cole didn't like to advertise it. He had been trained by the Fae themselves, and with his unnatural ability to use his axe more effectively than most, he was lethal.

Cole lengthened his strides. "With time running out on us, why don't we tackle the obvious first? Let's see what the lord of the castle has to say."

They walked from the crowded village down the main road toward the castle. The road twisted, and many times the trees from the forest on either side of the road obstructed their view.

With just the slightest touch to Gabriel, he stepped into the forest as the castle came into view. Gabriel would scout the castle while he talked to the baron.

Cole gazed at the massive wooden gate that was shut and the two guards that stood outside. As he passed villagers that were turned away, he began to wonder why the baron kept his castle sealed off to his villagers.

"What business do you have here?" one guard asked as Cole approached.

"I'm a knight from a distant castle. I've heard great things about your baron and wish to offer my services."

"We have plenty of knights."

Cole inhaled deeply and crossed his arms over his chest. "Shouldn't that be the baron's decision?"

The two guards looked at each other and laughed. "Unless you have an invitation from the baron himself, you don't gain entry into the castle."

Cole stared at the pair of guards before dropping his hands and turning on his heel to walk away. Half way back to the village Gabriel joined him on the road.

"Something isn't right here," Gabriel said.

Cole glanced over his shoulder to see more villagers turned away from the massive castle gates. "Aye. What lord doesn't allow his own people inside his walls?"

"One that has something to hide."

Cole nodded. "And the quickest way to discover what he has to hide is through his villagers." He turned to Gabriel to see his silver eyes alight with anticipation. "You have a plan."

"I have a plan," he said and quickly turned toward the village.

CHAPTER TWO

Shannon O'Malley seethed. Never in her life had she ever felt so alone – or weak.

Her chest still heaved from her frantic escape from the upstairs window. She had nearly made it too, but then Benton had suddenly appeared to stop her.

Yet again.

Benton Ducre. She hated the name as much as she hated the man. He held her prisoner, forcing her to work, and always keeping a close eye on her. Even at night, she had a guard outside her room.

The man was becoming a serious pain in her ass.

Why it was so important that she stay within reach at all times, she had no idea. All she knew was that one minute she had been minding her own business driving down the Chicago streets, and then the next, she was standing in thirteenth century England.

"Anon, wench!"

Shannon jerked at the voice behind her. Her eyes stung with unshed tears, her face throbbed where

Benton's meaty fist had slammed into her, and her pride was bruised from not having made her escape after careful planning for two weeks.

She was hanging onto her sanity by a thin thread that had already begun to unravel. If she ever made it back to her time, she was going to need serious psychological help.

With shaky hands, she reached for the mug of ale Benton had filled. Just as her hand closed around the thick mug, Benton's closed around hers. His dark, hooded eyes glared at her. She stared at his square face, flat nose, and protruding brow, and all she wanted to do was run. He was a mobster.

Oh, they might not be in Chicago, Hell, they weren't even in the twenty-first century, but he was a mobster.

"If you ever try that again…" His gravely voice trailed off.

She looked into his beady black eyes and shivered. He didn't have to finish the threat. She knew exactly what would happen to her.

With a jerk, she wrenched her hand out of his, sloshing ale over the both of them. Her legs grew steadier with each step she took away from the bar, but the rage only increased. She would make Benton and his cronies pay if it was the last thing she did.

"About bloody time," the man said when she delivered his ale.

She swallowed the bile that rose upon noticing his blackened teeth and greasy hair. It was just one of the many reasons she hated this hellhole she was in. She wanted to return to her century where people bathed, brushed their teeth, and maintained general hygiene.

As she turned away, he grabbed her hand. What was it with everyone grabbing her? She wanted to scream. Didn't anyone follow a personal space rule in this century?

"A nice set of tits ye have there," Greasy said as he hauled her onto his lap. "With those tits in me face, I could forgive ye anything."

Shannon guessed that most women would have been glad to receive such a compliment, but all she wanted to do was elbow him in the mouth. She tried to squirm out of his lap, yet he held on like a dog with a bone.

He laughed in her ear, his vile breath choking her. "Ah, ye like the feel of me pecker against yer backside, aye?"

Shannon stilled instantly. She glanced at Benton, and there must have been something on her face to alert him that she was fast loosing control because he hurried around the counter and pulled her out of Greasy's lap.

"Enough, Thatcher. Your wife is waiting for you," Benton said.

She watched as the man's smile vanished at having her yanked from his lap. She wondered if there might be a fight, giving her another chance at escape.

"Ye've never stopped us before, Benton," Greasy said as he slowly stood.

Benton glared at the man until Greasy sank back into his chair. "This is my tavern, Thatcher. What I say goes. If you don't like it, leave."

Shannon started to back toward the door when

Benton turned his black eyes on her as if he knew exactly what she was thinking. She hurried away, not caring what else Benton had to say to the man.

A woman could only take so much of the abuse every day without any answers to her questions before she turned like a caged animal and began attacking.

Her feet moved her to the back room under the stairway. It was a storeroom of sorts, but it was her room. No sooner had she closed the door behind her than Benton yanked it open and followed her in.

"Did I not hit you hard enough, wench?"

"I have a name," she ground out.

He growled and stepped towards her. "Answer me."

"What do you want from me?"

"To act like you're supposed to," he bellowed.

Shannon began to laugh. It was either that or cry, and crying in front of Benton the Beast was unthinkable.

His black eyes narrowed on her. "And just what do you find so humorous?"

"You," she said between laughs that now had her doubled over.

Apparently Benton didn't find anything amusing because he hauled her up by her hair, pulling off the little white cap he made her wear and scattering the pins that kept her hair in place.

She yelped and grabbed hold of his hand to stop him from pulling any harder.

"You'll act like a proper bar wench. You'll flirt with the men, let them fondle you and even fondle them yourself," he spat in her face. "Do you understand?"

She shook her head and blinked away tears. "Tell me why you weren't surprised to find me standing in the middle of the field."

He flung her away and strode to the door. "Keep those questions to yourself, wench. You'll find out the answers soon enough."

Shannon waited until the door closed behind him before she rose up on an elbow and swiped away the stray tear that had managed to escape.

Slowly, she climbed to her feet and found the poor excuse for a mirror on the wall. Her cheek hurt so badly that she could hardly move her mouth. Even in the dingy mirror, she could see the bruise forming on her right cheekbone.

With a sigh, she pushed her hair away from her face. Pins littered the floor, and she stared at them for a moment. Maybe if she refused to bathe, brush her hair or change her clothes Benton would no longer make her work the tavern floor.

Without another thought to her wild, tangled hair, Shannon walked out of the small room.

Cole spotted her instantly. She moved with the grace of a caged animal, one that was ready to strike at any moment. Her honey brown eyes flashed with anger and resentment wherever they landed.

She was being kept against her will.

As much as it was Cole's nature to help the less fortunate and weak, he knew he couldn't aid her. Not yet. Once they had vanquished the creature, then he could return and set her free.

He had seated himself in the back corner where the shadows kept most of him hidden. There, he could watch everyone and listen as the men talked.

It became harder and harder though as the woman kept drawing his attention. Each time she went to a table to deliver drinks or food, he was given a glorious view of her ample breasts, and despite the disarray of her brunette locks scattered around her, she looked positively sinful.

The kind of sinful that had him thinking of bed sport. All night bed sport.

When his mind turned to ways he wanted to claim her, he had to forcibly turn it back to the mission.

"Can I get you anything?"

Cole cursed silently at not noticing her before she walked to his table. He had been so deep in thought about forgetting her that he hadn't been paying attention.

With everything hinging on the fact that everyone needed to believe him a drunk, he raised his eyes, a goofy grin on his face as he pretended not to be able to focus on her.

Even acting drunk he couldn't help but notice her oval face, full lips, pert nose, and gently arching brows over eyes that slanted upwards at the corners. She was a beauty, and one he wanted desperately in his bed.

"Hold still, and I might answer you," he said, making sure to slur his words.

"You're drunk," she said, not hiding the loathing from her voice.

Her accent was like nothing he had encountered

before. She wasn't from England, Scotland, or France to be sure.

"Aye, darlin', I am. A man has that right every once in awhile," he drawled and took a drink, careful to make sure some spilled. "I'm nearly empty," he said as he smiled up at her and set the mug down. "I'd like another."

She put her hand on her hip and stared at him. "You should probably get home to your wife while you can still stand."

Cole laughed. "Ah, but I don't have a wife. I'm just drinking for the hell of it."

Her face softened, and her full lips pulled as if in a smile. She turned to glance over her shoulder, and that's when he saw the bruise. The entire right side of her face was turning a nasty shade of purple.

He clenched his left hand under the table and promised himself the man would pay for hitting her. It was the lowest kind of man that would strike a woman or child.

"Please, darlin'. I'm dying here."

She shook her head but went to the bar for his ale. While she had her back turned, he hastily emptied his ale in the corner. The woman was on her way back to him when Cole picked up on a conversation at a nearby table.

"Daniel, is it true? Did Marcus go missing last night?"

Daniel looked around and shushed the other man. "Not so loud. We don't want others to hear us, or we'll be next."

"Here you go," the woman said, cutting off the

conversation between the two men.

Cole smiled at her and reached into his coin purse to pay. "Here," he said, giving her more than enough.

She looked at the coins, then back at him. "It's too much," she whispered.

He shook his head. "The other is yours."

"I can't," she said and took his hand to give him back the coins.

Cole blinked at the tremor that went through him at her simple touch. His gaze jerked to her face to see if she had felt it too, but she didn't lift her gaze.

He refused to take the coin and moved his hand away from her grasp. "Where are you from?" he asked and sloshed more ale on the table.

She chuckled and wiped the spilled ale. "You're getting more on the table than in your mouth."

"I heard there were rooms to let here. Any available?"

For a long moment, she hesitated as if she didn't want to reply. Finally, she nodded her head.

"I'd like one."

She visibly swallowed, her slender throat begging for his kisses. "For how long?"

Cole shrugged, giving her that goofy grin again. "Depends. How long will it take?"

She straightened and put her hands on her hips. "For what?"

"To get you in my bed?"

She rolled her beautiful honey brown eyes. "Not in your wildest dreams," she mumbled before turning around.

"A week," he called out.

She waved over her shoulder letting him know she had heard him. He smiled to himself. She was going to be a handful for whatever man tried to claim her.

Shannon maneuvered her way back to the bar. After she had made arrangements for the customer's room, she realized she hadn't gotten his name. She was surprised to find she actually wanted to talk to him again.

Oh, he flirted with her like the others, but he didn't try to touch her, which was a huge difference in her book. He might be a drunk – and she abhorred drunks – but there was something about him, something different that drew her to him on a level she didn't quite understand.

It wasn't in the way he dressed, though his leather vest and shirt were of a different quality than the villagers. Not quite as nice as the baron's but not as plain as the poor.

Just...different.

Just as he was different.

She couldn't lay her finger on it, but surely given time she could discover what made him so unlike anyone else. She walked to his table. He was staring at it as if concentrating on something. The boyish smile and drunken charm he had oozed a moment ago had vanished, and in its place she saw the face of a warrior, the kind she saw in movies.

Then, in a blink, he raised his gaze and smiled at her. Her stomach fluttered with anticipation, an awareness of him she hadn't felt before swarmed her.

How she hadn't noticed his shoulder-length golden brown hair and chiseled face she didn't know. But as she took a closer look, she had to admit she liked his wide mouth, the blonde brows that slashed over his eyes, and his wide forehead.

If he wasn't drunk, she imagined he could be quite the looker. He was tall enough, and he obviously had the charm as he had shown in his smile and conversation.

But why did she even care? She wanted away from this time and back into her own.

Still, she couldn't deny the attraction she had to the man – intoxicated or not. His dark eyes met and captured hers, holding her enslaved by the desire she saw.

Desire? What the hell?

Shannon blinked and whatever emotion she thought she had seen in his gaze was gone. And somehow she was disappointed.

"Did you get my room?"

"I did," she answered after swallowing. "However, I need your name."

A slow smile spread across his face sending another jolt through her until her blood heated, and she could have sworn some dark, sinful promise flashed in his brown eyes.

"Cole de Gant. And yours?"

"Shannon. Shannon O'Malley."

"A beautiful name for a beautiful woman."

His compliment shouldn't have gone to her head, but it did. She wasn't a beauty, just…normal. Nothing about her stood out to catch men's attention.

She inwardly grimaced. That wasn't entirely true. She always attracted the wrong kinds of men. She wished she knew what it was that drew those men because she'd change it in a heartbeat.

To her amusement, Cole reached for her hand as if to kiss it and fell out of his chair. Unable to help herself, she laughed. He was an adorable drunk. He smiled up at her, a twinkle in his eye, as he rose up on an elbow.

She bent to help him up when rough hands seized her and threw her around and onto the floor. Dazed, and more than a little confused, she looked up to find men from the other tables gathered around them.

Shannon looked at the men, not understanding until one whispered 'outsider'. She was about to push back through the throng that had gathered around Cole to help him when she spotted a man carrying a dagger.

Before she could cry out, all hell broke loose.

CHAPTER THREE

The instant the men surrounded Cole, he shrugged off the drunk charade and leaped to his feet. He could see in the eyes of the men that they were hiding something.

"Get him and save one of our own," someone shouted just before they rushed him.

Cole was strong, but being encircled by nearly a dozen angry men left him at a disadvantage. But they had no idea he wasn't drunk, which gave him the upper hand. And enough time to ensure that it wasn't long before he was on equal footing with them.

With just a few punches and jabs, he knocked four men out. He never saw the dagger coming until it was too late. He shielded his face with his arm and felt the burn as the dagger sliced open his shoulder.

Years of training then took over. The Fae had taught him well, and he used every bit of that instruction to his advantage. He ceased to see faces, and concentrated on connecting his arms and legs to bodies.

When he next looked up, searching for his next victim, it took him a moment to realize he was the last man standing. He stood in the middle of bodies that lay sprawled on the floor, his breath coming in great gasps.

"Impressive," said a man standing beside Shannon, the same man who had hit her earlier. "Benton Ducre, owner of this establishment."

Cole nodded and started for the stairs. "Which room is mine?" he asked over his shoulder.

"Third on the right," Benton called out. "I thought you were drunk. I've never seen an inebriated man fight the way you just did."

Cole stopped and turned. "Fighting has a way of sobering a man."

Benton smiled. "That it does, my friend. I'll have food brought up to you."

Cole couldn't wait to get into his room. It was toward the end of the hall, which he liked, and he wasn't disappointed when he stepped inside. A table and two chairs sat near the hearth. The bed was on the opposite wall, and another smaller table stood next to it. There wasn't much to the room, but at least it was clean.

With the blood from his shoulder wound soaking into his tunic, he jerked the ruined garment over his head and reached for the looking glass. It took him a moment to adjust the glass to be able to see the cut.

It was just as he expected. Deep but not so deep that he would need the aid of Gabriel's herbs to help with the healing. Though he hated to admit it, Gabriel and his herbs would speed the process along.

As he looked at the cut, he realized that stitching it might not be a bad idea to stop the flow of blood and keep him from becoming weak.

After the attack downstairs, there wasn't such a thing as too careful, not when he needed all his strength to fight the evil.

He built up a fire and then cleaned his wound. He opened the small pack he always carried and found a needle for just such occasions.

It took him a moment to thread the needle and then situate the looking glass somewhere so that he could see into it in order to see what he was sewing. He didn't mind tending his own wounds, but he didn't want to be stitching skin that wasn't injured.

After several attempts, he was about to give up when there was a knock on the door.

"Enter," he said and watched as Shannon entered carrying a tray of food.

"Oh, my," she exclaimed and hastily set the tray down. "I had no idea you were hurt."

"It's just a scratch."

She raised her dark brows at him. "A scratch that is deep enough to need stitches? What am I thinking? You're right," she said with sarcasm dripping from her voice. "Just a scratch."

He smiled and nodded to the tray. "Thank you for bringing the food," he said and tried again to angle his shoulder so he could stitch it.

With a sigh, Shannon took the needle from him. "Let me," she said and pulled the other chair around so that she sat facing him. She glanced up and smiled.

"Trust me. I know what I'm doing."

He watched, mesmerized as she poured some of his ale over the needle before she moved to him. The shock of her soft, gentle hands on him startled him more than the needle that pierced his skin.

"Do you stitch many of Benton's customers?" he asked as a way to distract his mind and his growing cock to the violent, burning need to take her in his arms.

There was something in her honey brown eyes, honesty, courage, and...hope that stirred him.

He saw many things in women's eyes, but none had ever brought him up short as those in Shannon's did. She said the most unexpected things and did the most unexpected things, as well. Things a warrior would do.

And it made him yearn for her.

"Not hardly," she responded to his question

The scorn dripping from her voice left him smiling. "You never told me where you were from."

"Somewhere far, far away."

"Did you arrive in England on purpose?"

"No. It was quite by accident, but I'd love to return home."

Cole was curious as to why she was being held against her will. He wanted to ask her that and so many other things, but the soft wisps of her long, dark hair kept brushing against his bare arm and chest, driving him wild.

"Where are you from?"

For the first time in his life, he wanted to tell the truth. He wanted her to know who he really was. He wasn't sure why, but he knew the truth could kill him.

Instead, he told a half-truth. "I don't know. My family was killed when I was a small child. I was taken in by another family."

Shannon stopped sewing and raised her gaze to his. Their eyes caught and held. "I'm sorry. I shouldn't have pried."

He shrugged his good shoulder. "It's life."

She nodded and lowered her eyes to resume her work. "What brings you to this small village?"

"By accident," he lied. "I was traveling and ended up here. Why?" he asked with a grin. "Is there something I should know?"

"You know as much as I do," she mumbled right before she lowered her face to his arm.

Cole's entire body jerked at the feel of her soft lips on his skin. His body came alive, and the need, the unimaginable longing to have a woman in his arms was as strong as the need to breathe. But not just any woman would do.

He wanted Shannon.

"There," she said and straightened after biting off the thread. "You're all done."

He feasted his eyes on her face. She had a pert little nose and a stubborn chin, high cheekbones and a mouth made for kissing. She was, to put it plainly, exquisite.

He had the urge to reach up and smooth away the tendrils of hair that were tangled around her face, yet he controlled himself. Barely.

Cole reached for the looking glass and examined her work. The neatness of the stitches surprised him, as did the tightness of them as if she worried it might leave a scar.

"It's very good work," he said and watched her smile brighten at his compliment.

She shrugged as if it meant nothing. "If you ever find you need someone to bandage you, you know where to find me."

He flexed his injured arm and threw a grin at her as she rose. When she was about to turn away, he caught her hand.

Her eyes jerked to his face. He searched her depths for something, anything that would stop the lust searing his veins. Instead, he found fear and sorrow.

"Thank you," he whispered.

Her gaze dropped as she gently pulled her hand from his grasp. Cole allowed her to move away when all he wanted to do was pull her into his arms and taste her lips, to sink into her heat and ride the blissful pleasure he knew they would share.

She looked over her shoulder once more just before she opened the door.

Shannon didn't want to leave. It was the first time since her "appearance" in England that she truly felt as if she might have found a friend. But she knew Benton would keep a close eye on her.

Still, knowing that and finding him standing outside Cole's room surprised a gasp out of her. She knew how hard he could hit, and had seen men the size of Cole run from Benton. She didn't wish to see Cole hurt, so she hurriedly tried to explain herself.

"I was just coming down."

"You've been up here a mighty long time," Benton drawled as his eyes moved past her to Cole.

Shannon's mind whirled with possible explanations, then she decided on the truth. "He was cut. I know how you hate to have blood on the floors, so I stitched him."

She knew her words tumbled out fast, but once they started, they wouldn't stop. Her hands shook as she waited for Benton to respond.

She didn't dare look at Cole, for if Benton thought she cared what happened to him, Benton would kill him just for spite.

The sound of movement behind her drew her attention. She squeezed her eyes closed, wishing Cole would stay where he was and not interfere. Didn't he realize she was trying to save him?

"Is there a problem?" Cole asked from behind her.

Benton inhaled deeply as he crossed his arms over his chest. "Actually, there is. You've kept Shannon from her work, which has cost me coin."

The curiosity was too much for Shannon. She stepped to the side so she could see both Benton and Cole. The hardness of Cole's face alerted her to just how angry he was. His dark brown eyes flashed dangerously. With his high forehead, dark brows and square jaw and chin, she doubted Cole was a man people ever questioned.

Shannon raked her eyes over his wide, muscular shoulders, abdomen that could compete with a washboard, pecs that any body builder would envy, and arms that rippled with muscles. Even his neck was corded with muscles that his shoulder length golden brown hair grazed.

Her gaze was drawn to his lips. Wide, full lips that

had smiled playfully at her just moments ago were now pressed firmly together as he regarded Benton with...distaste.

"How much?" Cole finally spoke.

A slow, wicked smile spread over Benton's thickly bearded face. Shannon shuddered at the smile and wished Cole would just bash his head in so she could escape and be done with it all.

"Ten crowns."

Shannon felt the blood drain from her face. Even she knew it was an extraordinary amount, yet somehow she wasn't surprised when Cole reached into his pocket and pulled out the coins to hand to Benton.

Benton tossed the coins in the air and caught them, giving Cole a sneer. "My kind of man."

The tension was electrifying, and Shannon knew it was about to explode. Cole might be able to take Benton and a few of the other men on at once, but she knew how many men Benton had waiting for something just like that to happen.

"Let's get back downstairs," Shannon said and tried to push Benton out of the room.

Out of the corner of her eye she saw Benton raise his fist and knew it was going to land on her face. She braced herself expecting another agonizing slice of pain.

Then there was nothing.

She opened her eyes to find Cole had a hold of Benton's arm as the two men glared at each other.

"I would appreciate it if you no longer hit her," Cole ground out between clenched teeth.

Benton yanked his arm loose. "'Tis none of your

concern. Remember that, or next time you won't be left standing."

Before Shannon could look at Cole, she was jerked out of the room and down the stairs.

Cole kicked the door closed as one of Benton's men took a step toward him. With the way he felt, a fight was just what he needed. He waited, hoping the man would open the door, yet it stayed shut.

With a growl, Cole turned toward the table and his now cold food. It was time to find Gabriel anyway, so he locked his door, donned another tunic, and slipped out the window.

CHAPTER FOUR

Cole walked soundlessly between the buildings until he came to the spot where he was supposed to meet Gabriel. Just as expected, Gabriel was waiting, casually leaning against a tree as if he didn't have a care in the world.

In some ways, Cole envied him. Gabriel remembered nothing of his past life, not where he came from, how old he was, if he was immortal. Nothing.

To not have memories was better than to have glimpses as Cole did. Some nights he would dream of a beautiful lady with light brown hair he wound around his fingers as she sang to him. He had no idea if it was his mother or something his mind conjured to torture him.

Either way, he was tormented.

Gabriel nodded in greeting as he came to stand beside him. Cole's eyes scanned the sleepy village then moved to the castle. Torches lit the castle wall and towers as if it had just now come alive.

"Anything happen?" Cole asked.

Gabriel shook his head. "Not yet. Some movement at the castle, but nothing I can really see."

Cole flexed his aching shoulder.

Gabriel's eyes narrowed. "What happened?"

"Small fight in the tavern."

Gabriel turned toward him. "Let me see."

Cole lifted his tunic so Gabriel could examine the wound. Images of Shannon's tender hands as they stitched the cut and her soft mouth as she bit off the thread replayed in his mind. He wondered what she was doing now, and if Benton had dared to touch her once they left his chamber.

There wasn't much Cole could do anyway. Not now at least. Once he was through hunting though, then Benton had better pray for his life.

"Who stitched you?"

Cole, never one to keep things from the other Shields, found himself not wanting to share Shannon just yet. "A bar maid."

"She did an excellent job," Gabriel said. "I wish I'd have been able to mix some herbs to put in the wound before she stitched it, but I have something else to give you that will help it heal faster."

Cole nodded his thanks as he lowered his tunic. "We've got movement," he said and jerked his head toward the castle.

He and Gabriel quickly palmed their weapons and moved soundlessly through the trees for a closer look at the castle. They stopped just short of the gate when Gabriel held his hand up, halting their progress.

"Do you hear that?" he asked Cole.

Cole closed his eyes and listened. It was faint, but he heard the deep growl and what sounded like a hoof pawing the earth.

"The creature?" he asked.

Gabriel shrugged. "Could be. We won't know until we see it."

"Whatever it is, it's big."

"Aye," Gabriel agreed as he listened again to the animal. "Shall we take a closer look?"

Cole smiled. "I thought you'd never ask."

They circled the enormous castle, keeping to the shadows and out of the view of the guards that roamed the battlements and outside of the castle wall. Toward the back of the castle, the growling and pawing they heard became louder, more intense.

Not daring to utter a sound to alert the guards, Cole motioned to Gabriel that he wanted to see what it was. Gabriel nodded in agreement, and the two men reached up and began to scale the high stone wall.

Cole's fingers dug into the rocks, and he used the tips of his boots to help maintain his balance. He and Gabriel had scaled more difficult rocks, but the sheer height of the castle wall made the climb tedious.

Gabriel reached the top first and peeked his head over the edge. He glanced at Cole, giving the all clear before he went over the side. Cole pulled himself over the top with his arms and laid flat on the stones as a guard drew near.

Cole held his breath and looked down to find that Gabriel had reached the bottom and hid in the shadows, his bow ready to fire an arrow if need be.

Thankfully, the guard didn't see Cole, and once his back was turned, Cole hurried over the side and climbed down. When his feet touched the ground, he found himself facing a large wooden enclosure. He turned to Gabriel and spotted a guard advancing on them.

Without hesitation, Cole palmed his dagger and hurled it toward Gabriel. His fellow Shield didn't blink as he hit the ground on his stomach.

Cole smiled when his dagger landed in the heart of the guard who fell silently to the ground. He retrieved his dagger as Gabriel climbed to his feet.

A nod was exchanged between the two men. Thanks wasn't needed since they had each saved each other's hides more times than they could count. Instead, they focused on discovering just what was inside the enclosure.

A loud growl stopped them in their tracks. They quickly molded themselves to the wooden structure and waited. That's when they heard the voice.

"Don't forget 'twas you who called me," said a deep, obviously male voice that was almost more animal than human.

The male voice that responded was more cultured, belonging to someone of the nobility. "I haven't forgotten. I'm just waiting for the right time."

Cole moved and tried to peer through the cracks in the structure. Though the break was decent sized, he could only see an enormous fire and the bright red cloak of someone who paced slowly from one side of the structure to the other.

"My hunger grows. You know you shouldn't deny

me. To wait would be disastrous. Especially for you."

Cole saw Gabriel move to their left and around the back of the construction. Maybe he would garner a better look at the deep voiced man, but Cole would stay and see if he could identify the other voice, though he had a suspicion it was none other than the baron.

The man in the red cloak stopped his pacing and placed his hands on his hips. "I feed you."

"Not nearly enough," came the reply, followed by a ferocious roar.

If Cole didn't know better, he would say it was an animal speaking. He shook his head and looked again at the man in the red cloak. He could see his well-polished boots and the sleeves of his black tunic, but something blocked his view of the man's face.

Cole cursed and was about to move to a better spot when he heard a shout from the battlements.

"Guard down," men yelled.

Cole turned and found Gabriel moving toward him. Their time had run out. They would discover no more this night. Without a word, they hurriedly scaled the stone wall again. Just as Cole swung his legs over to begin his descent, he saw the man in the red cloak run out of the structure.

"Another time," Cole whispered as he followed Gabriel down.

They quickly used the thick brush of the forest to keep them hidden as the castle gate gave a loud creak that echoed through the night as it was opened.

Gabriel followed Cole back to the tavern. Before they spoke, they looked around for anyone who might be listening or who might have followed them.

When all was clear, Gabriel took a deep breath and looked at the moon. "We have little time."

"I know. I heard the gate opening. The guards will be looking for us."

"What did you see?"

"Not much," Cole answered. "I saw a cloak the color of blood, polished boots, and heard a voice of the nobility, but no face. You?"

For long moments, Gabriel didn't speak. Then he said, "I'm not sure what I saw."

That got Cole's attention. "Tell me."

Gabriel's silver eyes flashed in the moonlight as they turned to Cole. "I saw horns."

"Horns? Horns like the gargoyle we slew?"

Gabriel shook his. "Horns as thick as your bicep on either side of a head."

Cole rubbed his chin as he thought about what Gabriel saw. "Could it have been a helm like the Vikings wore?"

"Could be. Could also explain the dark cloak of fur he wore."

Cole snorted. "What in the world would the baron be doing consorting with a Viking?"

"The more important question would be how a Viking came to be in the thirteenth century."

"Magic," Cole said.

"Aye, magic, and if there is magic, you can guarantee that the blue stone has been found."

Cole nodded. "Aye, but if they called up a Viking, he'll be easy to kill."

"That's just it," Gabriel said as he crossed his arms over his chest and leaned against the wall of the inn.

"The creatures we have fought before have been so powerful and deadly that it has taken the special weapons of the Fae to kill them. Why call up a simple Viking."

Cole hated that he had a point. "I have a feeling that this man is more than a simple Viking."

The men exchanged a look.

"We need Aimery," Gabriel said.

Cole didn't waste any time. He called out to Aimery, a call that only the Fae could hear. In less than a heartbeat, Cole felt the unmistakable presence of a Fae. He didn't alert Gabriel though, preferring to have a little fun with his brother-in-arms.

"Have you information?" Aimery asked from behind Gabriel.

In a blink, Gabriel had drawn two of the daggers he kept on him and spun around, ready for battle. When he spotted Aimery, he cursed long and low as he put away his daggers in his leather jerkin.

Gabriel then turned his unusual silver eyes to Cole. "You knew."

It wasn't a question. Cole gave a slight nod.

"Well?" Aimery asked again.

Cole turned to the Fae commander, a Fae more powerful than any in the realm other than the king and queen. Aimery's Fae blue eyes shown eerily in the moonlight, and his flaxen hair flowed freely down his back, only pulled away from his face by small braids in intricate designs that hung to his shoulders.

"Nothing concise yet," Gabriel finally answered. "We have, however, seen something that we question."

Aimery looked from Gabriel to Cole. "What did

you see?"

"What looks to be a Viking," Gabriel said.

Aimery's smooth features furrowed in a frown. "A Viking?"

Cole nodded. "Why would the controller of the blue stone call up a Viking?"

"It was my understanding that they didn't have control over just what came out of the hole," Aimery said thoughtfully. "Have you found where the creature sprang from?"

"Nay," Gabriel said. "We arrived just today."

Aimery looked at the sky. "Night time and no attack. Strange. Too strange. Something is afoot here."

"Aye," Cole said. "Not that I'm doubting the Fae, but are you sure you sent us to the right time and place?"

Aimery's eyes narrowed, his swirling blue eyes growing dangerous. "We Fae do not get these things wrong. The creature is here."

"Then he hasn't been released yet," Gabriel said. "The village did not look like one that had been attacked and slaughtered. They walked around this morning as if they didn't have a care in the world."

"Yet," Cole interrupted, "in the tavern, I overheard something from two men. Apparently, people have been disappearing."

"Isn't that interesting," Gabriel said as he tapped a finger on his chin.

"Disappearing from where?" Aimery asked.

Cole shrugged. "Wasn't able to discover that, but I will by tomorrow."

"I want an update immediately," Aimery said.

Before Cole could answer him, he heard Gabriel clear his throat and turned his head to see a woman walking toward him. Cole had never seen the woman before, but he knew that look in her eyes – she wanted him.

And if it were any other time, he would have probably ushered her to his room. After all, his body was in need, especially after being tempted by Shannon.

It was both a gift and a curse that Cole had. Women wanted him. Always had. He loved the pleasure they gave him almost as much as the pleasure he gave them. He didn't need to even look at them to have them yearning for him.

And he never turned them down. He loved women. All women. Their resilience, beauty, and graceful bodies always amazed him. Women were extraordinary and deserved to be treated as such, and during the time he spent with them, however short, he tried to make them feel special.

Yet, tonight, the thought of being with this woman didn't appeal to him. Not even when she rubbed her ample breasts against his chest and cupped his rod.

His balls jerked hungrily, but as he gazed down into the woman's blue eyes, he hungered to see honey-brown eyes and brunette hair in disarray around a beautiful oval face.

He smiled down at her and gently removed her hand from between his legs.

"Another time," he said and placed a kiss on her forehead.

"A man like you turning down a night of pleasure?

I cannot believe that, milord."

"Ah, you are tempting," he lied, "but I have other duties to see to this night."

The woman pouted for just a moment before raking her gaze over him. "I'll be around."

Cole waited until she walked away before he turned to Gabriel and Aimery. He knew what was coming and didn't look forward to it.

"It amazes me every time," Gabriel murmured. "The only time I've ever seen anyone not look at a Fae is when you're around."

Cole shrugged and smiled. "What can I say? I'm irresistible."

Aimery chuckled and folded his arms across his chest. "You can dally all you want after we find the creature. Now, I need to go and see how Val and Roderick are coming along in the future."

Cole and Gabriel had no sooner nodded then Aimery was gone. It was one trick Cole wanted to learn. Despite being raised with the Fae, he didn't have that ability.

"I'll keep an eye out at the castle," Gabriel said and looked at the imposing structure again. "I've a feeling we'll find what we need there."

Cole nodded and saw movement out of the corner of his eye. He recognized Shannon instantly. "Until tomorrow," he threw over his shoulder as he headed toward Shannon.

CHAPTER FIVE

Cole stayed in the shadows wanting to see what Shannon was about before he announced his presence. When he saw her throw out a bucket of water, he realized she was still cleaning. A glance inside showed she was the only one working as Benton sat before the fire drinking.

He stepped out of the shadows toward her and whispered her name. She jumped and covered her mouth with her hand as she stared at him.

"Cole?" she asked softly after she had removed her hand.

He nodded.

Her brow furrowed. "I thought you were in your room."

"I was. I'm out here now."

She sighed and rolled her eyes at his comment. "Well, I can see that."

"Do you always clean by yourself?"

She looked over her shoulder into the tavern and

shrugged. "It's one of the many things I do since I've been here."

"I know they're holding you against your will." He didn't know why he let her know that, but somehow it seemed right that she didn't feel so alone.

Her eyes grew large before she looked away. "I like you, Cole," she whispered solemnly. "A lot, and it's because of that that I'm asking you to stay out of my life. If you meddle, they will kill you."

"I'm hard to kill."

Shannon's heart skipped a beat at the confident smile that spread across his handsome face. For just a minute, she believed that he might be able to help, but she quickly remembered just who held her.

No. No one could help her. Not now. Maybe not ever.

She needed to get away from Cole. Every time she was around him she wanted to throw herself at him. She was drawn to him like she had never been drawn to another man. He oozed sex appeal.

And Cole's sex appeal was about to drive her insane. Despite her lack of practice in the sex department, she knew if she ever did make love to Cole that it would be terrific. Great even.

Her eyes raked over his tall, muscular form, and she licked her lips in appreciation of his rock hard, tall body.

It took barely a thought to dredge up the image of him standing before her with his chest bare, her hands skimming over all that warm flesh as she tended his wound.

How she had wanted to spread her hands over his

chest and learn every inch of him. His devastating smile and dark eyes only complicated her feelings even more.

She picked up the bucket she dropped and turned to retrace her steps when his hand reached out and stopped her. The heat from his touch penetrated her sleeve and raced up her spine like bubbles in a soda.

Slowly, of their own accord, her eyes rose to his. The night hid most of his face, but the light from a tavern window showed her enough to see his smile had been replaced by a look of determination.

"Before I leave, I *will* set you free."

His deep voice rippled over her like silk, his promise laced in every syllable.

She wanted to hold onto that vow with both hands, but she wasn't a fool. Cole was making a promise he couldn't keep. But there was no need to tell him that.

With her heart hammering in her ears and her body begging for a kiss, she gave him a nod and tried to walk away. Yet, he kept hold of her arm.

She knew better than to look into his gaze again, knew it would only make her want him more, but she did it anyway. And when he drew her to him until only the bucket stood between them, Shannon inhaled his scent, and it sent her heart racing.

Mystery, sandalwood, sex, and power. It radiated from Cole as if it were a part of him, and the more Shannon was around him, the harder it was for her to walk away.

When his head lowered, tingles of excitement raced over her body. Her eyes lowered to his mouth, a mouth she suspected could kiss as fluently as he spoke.

Her lips parted of their own accord, hoping, praying for his kiss.

Her eyes closed as he came closer, and her chest rose and fell rapidly as his heat engulfed her. When his cheek touched hers, she nearly melted on the spot. It was only because he held her arms that she managed to stay upright.

"Stay alive," he whispered in her ear, his warm breath sending chills of delight over her skin.

He pulled away, and Shannon instantly missed his scent and warmth. When she opened her eyes, it was to find him staring at her. She realized he was waiting on a response. She opened her mouth, but her voice was lodged in her throat. A fool she was for thinking he might kiss her.

She cleared her throat. "I will," she said and somehow managed to pull out of his grasp. She turned and headed toward the tavern, silently hoping he would stop her again, and this time kiss her.

Yet, he didn't. When she came to the door of the tavern, she glanced over her shoulder to find him gone.

Cole fisted his hands at his sides as he watched Shannon enter the tavern. He shook with need and cursed himself for not kissing her when he'd had the chance. He had seen her parted lips, the desire in her eyes.

She was his for the taking. So why hadn't he taken her?

She was different.

Cole closed his eyes and leaned against the building as he tried to gain control of his raging body.

"That's something I don't see every day."

Cole grimaced when he heard Gabriel's voice. He looked to his left and saw his friend beside him. "How much did you see?"

"Enough."

Which meant all of it.

"Who is she?"

Cole shrugged. "I know her name is Shannon, and she hasn't been here long. Her speech is different, but she won't tell me where she is from, just says it's far away."

"Interesting. If I'm not mistaken, that's the same girl we watched trying to escape earlier."

"The same."

"Interesting."

Cole ground his teeth. "Quit saying that."

Gabriel grinned and glanced in the tavern. "Well, it is interesting. I've watched you for many years around women. Always before, they are attached, and you aren't. Never have I seen what I saw just now."

"Don't," Cole warned dangerously. He didn't know what was going on, and he damn sure didn't want Gabriel asking questions.

"Calm down, Coleman," Gabriel cautioned in a low voice.

Cole squeezed his eyes shut. It wasn't like him to turn on a friend, especially a Shield. What the hell was wrong with him?

A hand gripped his shoulder. "Get some rest," Gabriel said. "We've a long day tomorrow."

Cole opened his eyes and sighed. "I'll meet you at dawn."

Gabriel said goodnight and faded into the darkness. For long moments, Cole watched Shannon as she cleaned. Part of him knew he should forget her, but another part of him couldn't, especially not after he had made her that promise--a promise he would fulfill.

When he could stand it no longer, he walked to the back of the tavern and climbed up to his room. Though he crawled into bed and shut his eyes, he knew he would get little sleep. Not with images of Shannon in his head.

He could still smell her exotic scent, see her honey-brown eyes heavy-lidded with desire, her lips parted as she waited for his kiss. He could well imagine her full breasts in his hands and her sex clenching around him as he thrust into her.

And it drove him wild with need.

Shannon woke the next morning more tired than she had been in ages. Mostly it was due to the fact that her mind was full of Cole.

He was as mysterious a man as she would ever meet. A man who wouldn't give her the time of day in her own time, but a man who had promised to free her before he left.

Free her.

She sighed as she threw off the covers and climbed out of bed before Benton came in to get her. Her penchant for daydreaming ended the moment she arrived in this time.

Reality was a hard pill to swallow, but swallow it she must. After all, who would be looking for her in her own time?

Always she had been alone, and that was how she would stay until she died. As she pulled on the simple, coarse gown given to her, she couldn't help feeling that she wouldn't be alive for much longer.

Someone had brought her here, but to what purpose? So far, she had learned nothing, and how could she when she was kept in this hell hole twenty-four hours a day.

With a vicious yank, she pulled the comb through her hair to work out the tangles that always managed to appear overnight. Her hair was fortunately long enough that it was easy to pull back in a loose bun with the pins that were provided to her. It might not last through the day, but at least it would start that way.

Once her feet were in what sufficed for shoes, she opened the door and walked into the main room only to see...Cole. He stood leaning against the massive fireplace, his head down, with one hand on the stones and the other on his hip, as if he were deep in thought.

She drank in the site of his tall, muscled body, a body that men worked daily for but would never accomplish. His golden brown hair hung loose and wavy to his shoulders, begging her fingers to run through it.

All of a sudden, his head jerked up, and he slowly turned to look at her. Shannon's stomach fluttered before it dropped like lead to her feet. Neither made a move as they looked at each other across the room.

His gaze looked troubled. Shannon took a step toward him when Benton walked in front of her.

"Quit your dallying. There's work to be done," he ordered.

By the time he moved past her, Cole was gone. Shannon didn't like the empty void that filled her, and she quickly shook her head to clear it.

Or she tried.

Despite her attempts, Cole's image stayed with her throughout the morning. There had been something in his eyes, something that had alerted her, and she wanted to know what it was.

And so she began to plan.

CHAPTER SIX

Cole made himself leave the tavern. He told himself not to wait around in the main room, but he had stayed, hoping to catch a glimpse of Shannon after a night full of dreams.

Dreams of her dying...in his arms.

He had woken in a foul mood, a mood that would only dispel at seeing Shannon with his own eyes. Yet, his mood hadn't lifted at seeing her. Instead, it intensified. He needed answers about why she was here, why she was being held, but even he knew those would have to wait until he and Gabriel found the creature and destroyed it.

And Cole feared that by then, Shannon would be dead.

When he found Gabriel behind the building, he walked past his fellow Shield toward the castle. "Did you discover anything last night?" he asked.

"Good morn to you as well," Gabriel said as he caught up. "Did you not sleep well?"

"Nay," Cole murmured. "I didn't."

Gabriel's hand on his shoulder stopped him. "Tell me."

Cole looked closely at his friend before raking a hand through his hair. "Dreams, Gabriel. I had dreams." He thought his explanation would be enough, but he should have known Gabriel better than that.

"What kind of dreams?"

It was something in Gabriel's voice that drew Cole's attention. He watched Gabriel carefully as he said, "I see a woman dying. In my arms."

Gabriel blanched, and Cole knew his dreams were more than mere dreams. He took a step toward Gabriel. "What do you know?"

With a shake of his head, Gabriel turned away from him. "Those aren't just any dreams. Heed me well, Cole. Pay close attention to them. Who was the woman?"

"Shannon."

Gabriel whirled around, his silver eyes ablaze. "What is she to you?"

"I honestly don't know."

Gabriel watched Cole. As long as he had known him, Cole had never acted this way towards a woman. Women were women. Meant to be loved, then left, yet this Shannon had him all but tied in knots. And as far as Gabriel knew, Cole hadn't yet taken her to his bed.

"Listen to me carefully," he said to gain Cole's attention. "Go over those dreams one by one. There will be something in them that can help us."

"Help us with what?"

"Save her. You were shown those dreams for a reason. We're not just going to sit by and let her die when there's a way to save her."

Cole closed his eyes and lowered his head, but not before Gabriel saw the relief in them. He had no idea how much time they had to work with, and add to that finding whatever creature they were to hunt and kill.

But he would do what he could to aid Cole since even a blind man could see how disturbed he was. Though Gabriel wouldn't admit it, he knew just what kind of dreams Cole was having. They weren't dreams. They were nightmares that had haunted Gabriel for years.

"Thank you," Cole said as he raised his head.

Gabriel started towards the castle. "Don't thank me yet."

Cole wished the creature would show itself. Knowing what they were going up against would alleviate some of his anxiety. He hated the waiting, especially when his mind was occupied with something else.

His hands itched to feel his weapon in them as he swung it at the creature. What would it be this time? Another gargoyle, a giant snake? A three headed dog?

Patience wasn't a virtue given to him, and no amount of teaching from the Fae had ever lent him the ability to master it.

"We need to get into the castle," Gabriel said as he watched as more people stopped at the castle gates only to be turned away.

Cole chuckled and slapped him on the back. "Why didn't you say so sooner?"

"You have an idea?" Gabriel's eyes crinkled in the corners as he looked at Cole.

"I have an idea."

Nearly three hours later, Cole and Gabriel walked solemnly toward the castle gate.

"I hope this works," Gabriel hissed.

Cole sighed. "It'll work. Have faith, my brother."

"It better."

Cole kept his head bowed as they stopped in front of the guards at the gate.

"State your business," the guard demanded.

"What do you think the business of a monk is, my son?" Cole asked.

The guard sneered and motioned to the men above him to open the gate. "A fat lot of good you monks do," the guard murmured as they walked past him.

Cole and Gabriel walked through the gate as if they had all the time in the world. Cole could literally feel Gabriel's tension. They stopped once they reached the bailey and discreetly looked around from beneath the hoods of their cloaks.

"Where would you like to begin?" Cole asked.

"The Viking. If he is indeed a Viking."

They smiled to each other and moved in the direction they had been the previous night. The building was empty, and no one stopped their entry.

But to their disappointment, there was nothing for them to see.

But Cole wanted a closer look.

"Keep watch," he said as he walked into the wooden building.

Whoever had built it had done it in a hurry. It was roughly put together, as if they didn't expect to use it long. He studied the ground, and saw it had all but been trampled. Whoever had been in here had done much more pacing than what they had witnessed last eve.

His eyes scanned the area, searching for anything that might give him some clue about the Viking. He was just about to give up when he spotted what looked like claw marks in the wood. He ran his fingers along the marks, noting how long and wide they were.

He turned and walked back to the entrance.

"Find anything?" Gabriel asked.

"Aye. Claw marks."

Gabriel thought that over for a moment before he said, "So, the creature is here."

"Aye and he's big. Those marks were twice the size of my hand," Cole said and held up his large hand.

"A big one all right. So, it's like the gargoyle, only attacking at night?"

No sooner were the words out of his mouth than a roar split the silence. Cole and Gabriel watched as the few people inside the castle walls hurried to safety.

"I would say, nay," Cole said and scanned the bailey.

Gabriel threw him a look. "Where should we start?"

"I don't think we should. Not yet."

Gabriel's black brow went up in question.

"Oh, we'll hunt him, but I think we need more information. He hasn't attacked yet. I want to see just what we're dealing with."

"You may be right. We know where he is, and we know how to gain access to the castle if we need to return."

"Exactly," Cole said. "I say we return to the village and question more of the people. Someone will talk."

"Good idea. I'm not comfortable in these monk's robes."

Cole hid his grin as they walked back to the gate and toward the village. After the road turned and put the castle out of view, they ducked into the trees and made their way to the tavern. They threw off the monks' cloaks, and Cole tossed his to Gabriel who would hide them for future use.

"All right," Gabriel said as he adjusted his clothes. "Where do we start?"

"The tavern."

Cole knew Gabriel thought he wanted to return because of Shannon, and maybe part of him did, but the other part realized drunken men talked the easiest.

"I'll go first," was all Gabriel said.

Cole waited as long as he could before he followed Gabriel into the tavern. He spotted his friend sitting in a back corner near a group of men that were well into their cups.

He was making his way to the table he preferred when he spotted Shannon. She was being groped by a group that wanted more than food and drink. Try as she might, she wasn't able to get them to release her.

Without thinking, Cole realized he moved toward her. He watched as she elbowed one man in the face when he latched onto her breast. The man shoved her away from him while another man stuck out his foot and tripped her.

Cole saw her falling as if in slow motion and realized she would hit her head on the corner of a table. In two strides, he was beside her, catching her before she could bang her head.

She looked up into his face, her eyes round with fear. He smiled, hoping it would help calm her.

"You caught me," she whispered.

"I did."

For a long moment, she simply stared at him, giving Cole time to memorize the feel of her warm, wonderfully curvy body in his arms. Her full breasts were pressed against his chest, and he wanted nothing more than to carry her up the stairs to his room and make slow, sweet love to her until she forgot everything but him.

"Thank you."

Her words jerked him to the present, and he realized he needed to release her. He righted her and backed away with a nod.

He cursed himself as he made his way to his table after having drawn every eye in the tavern his way. With controlled movements, he pulled out the chair and slowly sank into it. He fisted his hands beneath the table wishing he had smashed his fist into the men who dared touch Shannon.

After a deep breath, he had steadied himself

enough to rest his forearms on the table. He closed his eyes and opened his ears to hear snatches of conversations around him.

"...ever since she came ...."

"...gotten worse, I tell ye, and 'tis goin' to get even shoddier."

"...too many strangers. Take them, I say, instead of the people that have made this village their home."

"...she talks funny, too ...."

The smell of innocence, life, and freshness assaulted him. He didn't need to open his eyes to know who it was beside him.

Shannon.

"Yes."

His eyes snapped open. He hadn't realized he had spoken her name out loud.

"Here," she said as she placed a mug of ale in front of him. "I thought you might want this."

He refused to meet her gaze, afraid she would see the stark hunger in them for her. Instead, he kept his eyes on the table.

"Thank you," he managed past his dry mouth.

He let out his breath when she finally walked away, and when he lifted his gaze, it was to find Gabriel watching him. Those hawk-like silver eyes of Gabriel's missed nothing.

But Shannon and Gabriel vanished from his thoughts when he heard a man whisper something about a sacrifice. Cole leaned forward and tried to listen through the crowd of people all talking over the other.

"...who'll be next?"

"...I'm about ready to leave. Too many have died already."

Ah, so they haven't disappeared. They've died. But where? And how?

"...it'll happen tonight. You watch," said one old man whose hand shook as he said the words.

Cole watched as the others silently nodded, and as much as he yearned for more information, the quieter they became.

Nothing more was spoken of the dead or just what would happen tonight, but he knew he and Gabriel would be there to see what it was.

Just as he was about to go to his chamber, the door flew open, and a tall, well-dressed man in a blood red cloak sauntered into the tavern.

CHAPTER SEVEN

Cole knew instantly that the man was the lord of the castle. His hair was so black it shone blue, and his beady eyes missed nothing as they scanned the room. His nose was hawkish in style, and his face was lean and angular. He was slim, but Cole could tell there was strength in his body by the way he carried himself.

When the lord's gaze stopped on Cole, he stared him down, waiting to see what the man would do. To his delight, the baron walked his way.

Cole leaned back in his chair, and just as the arrogant lord reached the table Cole kicked the chair with his foot, sliding it out beside the baron.

"You're new here."

Cole nodded and looked at the chair. "Have a seat, and we can discuss anything you like."

For a moment, he didn't think the baron would take the chair, but in the end he did.

"What is your name?" the baron asked as he sank into the chair, his men surrounding the table.

"Cole."

"Cole?" he repeated. "No surname."

"Nay."

"Only bastards go without surnames."

The entire room gasped and waited for Cole's reaction. It was quite an insult to be called a bastard.

"And you are?" Cole said, unaffected by the baron's words.

"Baron Gyles Le Blanc."

Cole nodded. "Ah. A very important name."

"That goes along with a very important person."

"You want me to leave the village, I suppose."

Gyles sat back and leisurely looked Cole over. "From what I've heard, you caused a problem in here yesterday."

"Would you believe me if I said it wasn't my fault."

Gyles threw back his head and laughed. "I like you," he said and leaned on the table. "You may stay. For a while."

Cole lifted his mug of ale in salute and drank deeply. His dislike of the baron intensified with each passing moment. The baron was too cocky, too confident, and too evil not to be involved with the summoning of the creature.

After another hearty laugh, the baron rose and walked from the tavern. As one, the room seemed to sigh when the door closed behind Gyles.

Cole found Gabriel's gaze and knew they needed to talk. He watched as Gabriel rose from his table and exited the tavern. Cole drained his ale, laid money on the table, and then rose. He would leave by his chamber again. The last thing he wanted was everyone to realize he and Gabriel were together.

He opened the door to his room and stepped inside. After barring the door, he leaned against it and sighed. He missed having the Shields together, and he still mourned Darrick terribly.

They always traveled together. Or had. Until the creatures popping up everywhere intensified. They had no choice but to be split up, but in doing so, it weakened them.

Each man brought something different to the Shields, something that aided in their successes. Now with them being split, their chances of victory had lessened while the odds continued to stack in the evil's favor.

How Cole hated it.

A sound alerted him that he wasn't alone. His eyes scanned the room and found Shannon beside his bed. She twisted her hands as if agitated or frightened.

"Leave," she said. "Leave now and don't ever look back."

In two strides, he was beside her. He gripped her shoulders and made her look at him. "What do you know?"

"That you'll die."

"I'm not that easy to kill," he said with a smile.

She threw her hands out. "Stop it. Just stop it. This isn't a joke. Gyles is evil, and he will kill you."

"How do you know that?"

"Because he singled you out," she said, her voice low as if she had lost a major battle.

She needed to be comforted, and he needed to comfort her. He pulled her into his arms. The feel of her against him once again was like heat from the sun after a long, cold winter. Her arms eagerly wrapped around him as he held her, hoping to take some of her fear from her.

His body instantly came to life at her touch. Never did he know a need for a woman like what engulfed him at that moment. And no amount of telling himself there wasn't time for any dalliance would make his body listen.

He looked down to find her face tilted toward his, her mouth parted slightly as she licked those beautiful lips – and he was lost, drowning in passion so intense it made him forget everything and everyone around him.

Shannon saw Cole's brown eyes darken right before he bent his head and captured her lips. His kiss stole her breath as his passion rained down upon her. His hands roamed her body as if memorizing every inch of her. She plunged her hands into his silky hair and molded herself against him, feeling his hardness against her stomach and wishing for more as her sex clenched in need.

The kiss sent her spiraling into an abyss of desire that she had only read about in romance novels. The urgency in his kiss spurred her onward. He drained her of all emotion save one –passion.

She forgot about traveling to another time and continent, forgot being kept prisoner, and forgot that she was alone. Her entire being centered around Cole and the most erotic kiss she had ever experienced.

It awoke her body and desires she never knew she had. The intense feelings frightened her, but she didn't turn from them, couldn't turn from them.

Wouldn't turn from them.

When he ended the kiss and pulled away, she wanted to cry out for him not to stop. Instead, she let him hold her against his chest as she struggled to get her breathing under control. It helped to hear that his breathing wasn't any better than hers.

"I'm not leaving," he suddenly said.

She was ashamed to admit she was thankful he wasn't going. He was her only friend, the only person she could turn to if she were in need. If he left, she knew she wouldn't last long alone. She wasn't a strong person.

"Then don't prove me right," she said and stepped out of his arms to look into his dark eyes. She hated to leave, but she needed to return downstairs before she was missed.

Without a backwards glance, she walked from his room before she did something foolish like offer her body to him.

Cole stared at the door Shannon had just walked through. He wanted to go after her, to pull her back into his room and never let her leave.

He wanted to strip her of her gown and gaze upon her naked flesh. He wanted to run his hands, lips, and tongue over her entire body to learn what pleased her. He wanted to see her head thrown back in passion.

But most of all, he wanted her to want him with as much desire as he wanted her.

Suddenly, he realized he wasn't alone and turned to the window to find Gabriel in the shadows.

Before Cole could say anything, Gabriel held up his hand to quiet him. "I had no idea …."

"I know," Cole said and sank onto the bed, grateful to have something to take Shannon out of his mind before he went daft. "I take it you heard my conversation with the baron?"

"I did," Gabriel said as he walked to the table near the hearth and sank into one of the chairs. "Come. Your stitches need to be removed."

Cole was glad he didn't bring up the kiss with Shannon. He didn't think he could talk about it, not when the emotions she stirred within him were so raw.

He sat and removed his tunic so Gabriel could see to the wound. "I also heard bits of a conversation downstairs that revealed that the people aren't disappearing, but being killed," Cole said.

Gabriel reached for one of his small daggers and moved to the stitches. "Curious."

Cole nodded and waited for the stitches to be removed. Once Gabriel was done he tugged his tunic back on. "What's more curious, is that something is going to happen tonight."

Gabriel smiled and rubbed his hands after putting the dagger away. "About bloody time."

The moon was high in the sky when Cole and Gabriel finally saw movement. They set up watch between the castle and the village, and for many long hours, the night was as quiet as death.

Then the creaking of the castle gate reverberated in the darkness. Cole fingered his double-headed war axe, eager to begin the battle.

With nary a sound, Gabriel reached for one of his special arrows and notched it in his bow. Cole glanced at the tip of the arrow. It was a tip designed by the Fae, and was made like a mace with a small ball that had spikes all around it.

Cole counted twelve guards as they filed past them in two rows. The guards' weapons were numerous, as if they expected resistance of some kind.

He and Gabriel watched as the guards marched to the village. Without a word to the other, both men rose from their spots and raced after the guards. They reached the village in time to see the guards burst into a house and take a young girl, her parents trying desperately to touch her one last time, and their cries filling the night air.

Cole's ears rang from the screams, and the tears the girl and her family cried. He stepped forward to intervene until Gabriel stopped him with a hand on his shoulder.

"Why?" he asked, not believing Gabriel wouldn't want to save her.

"You don't know that this has anything to do with the creature."

"And you don't know that it doesn't."

Gabriel sighed. "Let us just see where they take her."

Reluctantly, Cole agreed. He looked about the small village to see if anyone watched, if anyone would dare to help the girl. Yet he saw no one.

Until his eyes found the tavern.

Shannon stood in the window, her hands pressed against the shutters. She needed to hide, and he was about to make her do just that when one of the guards spotted her.

"Won't be long now," he taunted her as he pulled the girl along behind him.

Cole's hand tightened on his war axe, eager to split the guard's head open. He saw Gabriel slip behind the building to retrace their steps, and for a moment, Cole debated whether to follow him or go after the guards himself.

It was a foolish thought, and Cole was anything but foolish. With a vile curse, he turned and followed Gabriel. He caught up with the other Shield just as Gabriel reached their hiding spot.

"Didn't think you were coming."

Cole sighed. "Almost didn't."

He felt more than saw Gabriel's stare in the darkness.

"We've never failed," Gabriel reminded him.

"We've never been split up before either," Cole replied.

There was no more time for conversation as the guards approached them.

"Please let me go," the girl begged. "I haven't done anything."

The guards laughed, and the one holding her jerked on the rope around her neck sending her to her knees. He continued walking, dragging the girl until she could regain her feet, which was difficult considering that her hands were tied in front of her.

"Of course you haven't done anything," the guard said with a sneer.

Cole tightened his grip on his axe. It wasn't until they neared the gate that the roar they heard earlier in the day sounded again – this time louder...and closer.

"What the bloody hell is that?" Gabriel whispered.

"The creature."

Gabriel grunted in response, readied his bow, and let loose the arrow. The arrow struck one of the back guards in the throat. He never made a sound as he fell to the ground.

Without missing a beat, Gabriel let loose three more in quick succession, freeing the girl. She tugged the rope from her throat, picked up her skirts with her tied hands, and raced back to the village.

While Gabriel prepared to fire three arrows at a time, Cole walked out onto the road and waited for the guards to see him. It didn't take long.

Gabriel let loose the three arrows, leaving the rest of the guards for Cole. He swung his massive axe over his head and let it fall, cleaving one guard in two.

He then pivoted, ducked a sword that was aimed at his neck, and imbedded his axe in a guard's abdomen. Cole kicked the guard off his axe as another attacked him.

Out of the corner of his eye, he watched as Gabriel's arrows took the remaining two out, leaving one for Cole. Cole and the guard circled each other. Whereas the guard was anxious, fearful, Cole was ready and eager for the fight. Holding his axe in both hands, he brought it up and broke the guard's nose with the handle.

The guard sputtered and cursed as he backed away, holding his nose while blood gushed through his fingers. Cole stood his ground as Gabriel moved beside him.

"You don't know what you've done," the guard said as another roar sounded.

"Then tell us," Gabriel said.

The guard retrieved his sword and shook his head. "Never."

Cole prepared to take the guard prisoner to make him talk, and as the guard rushed towards him, his sword raised, an arrow zoomed between Cole and Gabriel to imbed in the guard's heart.

Gabriel and Cole dove into the trees. Without a backward glance, they raced from the castle toward the village. Cole knew that whoever had killed the guard would be looking for them next.

He gave Gabriel a nod as they split up, and he snuck back into his chamber. With fingers aching, he hung outside his window for long moments, listening to make sure no one was inside waiting to ambush him.

When he heard nothing, he quietly slipped inside and inspected every inch of the room before he shed his clothes and weapons and lay atop the bed.

He didn't have long to wait before he heard banging on the front door of the tavern.

CHAPTER EIGHT

Shannon nearly jumped out of her skin when she heard the bang on the tavern door. Ever since the castle guards had taken the girl and then taunted her, she hadn't been able to think of anything other than getting away from the village.

Escape plans rushed through her mind only to end with her being caught. She couldn't leave on her own. She knew that now. Help was what she needed, and there was only one man who could aid her.

Cole.

The sound of men's voices intruded on her thoughts, and she wondered if her time to be taken to the castle had come. She had never seen the guards get more than one person at a time, but that didn't mean they wouldn't.

To her amazement, it wasn't to her door that the footsteps sounded, but up the stairs to stop directly above her. At Cole's room.

Her hands trembled, and her lungs stopped moving

as she listened for voices. Dimly, she heard faint steps, probably Cole's after he rose from his bed. All she could make out of the voices were one big mumble, and she nearly screamed her frustration.

For too long she had sat and done nothing, it was time to take matters into her own hands. On tiptoes, she walked to her door and eased it open until the slit was wide enough for her to slide through. She inched toward the stairs, and the voices became clearer, louder with each step.

"Where have you been?"

She heard Cole chuckle and could imagine him running his hand through his hair.

"I told you, I've been in my bed," Cole said.

"Sleeping?"

"Well, that is one thing a body does in bed," Cole replied.

Shannon leaned around the stairs to see the four guards crowded around Cole's door. It was one of the middle guards that said, "You don't look like you've been asleep."

"Like I said, the bed is for more than sleeping," Cole replied, his voice edgier than before.

Shannon was just about to step onto the stairs to lend Cole her aid when one of the other rooms opened and a beautiful woman with long blonde hair stepped out.

All four of the guards turned to see who it was, and parted as she walked toward Cole. Shannon's stomach fell to her feet when she saw Cole put his arm around the woman and smile at her. The look that passed between them was one only lovers shared.

"He's been with me," the woman all but purred up at Cole.

Shannon's eyes were riveted on Cole's face as he stared at the guards.

"Satisfied?" Cole asked.

All but one guard turned away, and before Shannon slipped back into her room, she heard him say, "For now."

A shiver raced down her spine at those words. She had no doubt the guards would return. But for her or Cole, she didn't know.

And one nagging question was unanswered, where was Benton? He wasn't the kind of man to let the guards question Cole alone. Benton would have been right there with them. So, where was the evil son of a bitch?

That's when it hit her.

Benton wasn't at the tavern. How many nights had she lain awake dreaming of ways to escape? How many nights had she paced her small room in hopes of one day leaving and never looking back?

How many nights had Benton left the tavern?

Anger seethed and grew in Shannon. Anger at herself for being fooled, and at Benton for fooling her.

But no longer. She had had enough.

She wasn't a slave, and she would no longer patiently wait for the day the guards took her to the castle for her death. Nor would she wait on someone to help her. She could do this herself. She would do this herself.

After she hurriedly dressed, Shannon slipped out of her room and went to the kitchen. She grabbed the longest, widest knife she could find and strapped it to her leg with pieces of cut leather. She then stuffed some food into a sack before she started for the back door.

She hesitated for just an instant, thinking she might speak to Cole, but then she remembered the woman in his arms and decided against it.

With a deep breath, she unlatched the door and walked into the night. The trees that would hide her were just twenty yards away. She made to take a step toward them when she heard the guards along the main street.

She would have to be careful. Benton might return soon.

That thought propelled her into action. She rushed into the trees, refusing to look back.

Finally. Finally!

The smile that pulled at her lips was the first in weeks, and the fear that she might never return to her own time was held at bay by her newfound freedom.

Gabriel waited until Shannon had reached the safety of the trees before he turned toward the tavern. He sighed as he picked up a small rock. He tossed the rock into the air and caught it. Repeating the motion several times, he thought over his options.

Cole needed to stay in his chamber in case the guards returned, but he knew Cole would have his head if he didn't tell him Shannon had left.

He gripped the small rock and thought of Hugh

and the love he had for Mina, a love most people could only dream about. Gabriel might fool other people into believing he didn't need or want anyone, but the truth was, he did.

With a sigh, he tossed the rock at Cole's window. In heartbeats, Cole had thrown open the shutters and leaned out. Gabriel motioned him down and waited.

"What is it?" Cole asked as he joined Gabriel. "Those guards could return at any time."

Gabriel stared at his friend for a long moment, once again wondering if he was doing the right thing. "Shannon has left."

Cole took a step back and looked up at the trees before dropping his head to his chest. When he raised his head, the warrior was back in place.

"I'm going after her."

"I assumed as much," Gabriel said.

Cole hurried back to his chamber where he dressed and retrieved his two small axes. He strapped them to each side of his hip, and strapped his double-headed war axe to his back.

He was going to be prepared for anything.

"I should've helped her," Cole said as he rejoined Gabriel. He was angry at himself for not seeing she needed to be free of this place.

"We do have another assignment. Besides, you promised her you'd help her leave."

"Looks like I'll be doing that sooner than I expected."

"Nay," Gabriel said. "We need her to return."

Cole stared at him, trying to determine what Gabriel meant. "Why?"

"She knows something is going on. We both saw her tonight, and I can almost guarantee that it wasn't the first time she's seen the guards take someone. She can tell us what we need to know. Besides, you know she hears more from the customers than we ever would."

Cole hated that Gabriel was right. The last thing he wanted was Shannon mixed up in this mess, not to mention his dreams of her dead in his arms. "I'll have to convince her. Which way?"

He didn't like the fear that raced through him knowing Shannon was on her own, that she hadn't waited on him to help her. He also didn't like the fact that he was going to have to persuade her to return to people who could very well plan to kill her. If the situations were reversed, Cole would tell himself to bugger off.

As he followed Gabriel, he pushed everything but finding Shannon aside. They covered more ground than she did and easily caught up with her. She ran as if the hounds of hell were after her. He admired her gumption to strike out on her own in a land she obviously didn't know, regardless of the dangers. Only her freedom mattered.

Suddenly, Cole heard something behind him and turned to find four castle guards following them. He grabbed the two small axes in each hand.

"Get her," Gabriel said before he stopped and crouched down in the tall grass as he readied his bow.

Cole was ever amazed at the accuracy of Gabriel and his bow, but there wasn't time to watch now. He turned back to Shannon and lengthened his strides. He couldn't chance calling out to her in case there were more guards, so Cole did the only thing he could – he tackled her to the ground.

To stave off some of the impact, Cole turned and took the brunt of the fall as he landed on his back. With a flick of his hands, he unlatched the strap that kept his war axe strapped to his back, and rolled on top of her to keep her knees from connecting with his manhood as she fought to free herself from his grasp.

"Enough," he whispered in her ear. "It's me. Cole."

She stopped struggling, and Cole slowly rose up, though he didn't loosen his hold on her arms.

"Why did you run?" he asked.

She looked away from him. "Benton wasn't there. I saw my chance and took it."

"I told you I would help."

The clouds covering the moon parted, allowing him to see her face. When her soft brown eyes met his, he saw the panic and desperation in their depths.

"I couldn't wait any longer," she replied softly.

Cole couldn't find the words to respond to her, especially once he realized he was atop her soft, lush body. He instantly recalled their passionate kiss, and his body reacted as if it hadn't had a woman in months. The urge to taste her again consumed him.

The hunger for her grew.

He had never craved a woman like he craved the taste of Shannon. Her silky skin beneath his hands made him itch to feel the rest of her, and her full breasts pressed against him only intensified his yearning.

His mouth was but breaths from hers, and it was

more than a normal man could stand. And he was by far anything but normal. His body cried out for him to take her, to taste her again, to make her his.

He inhaled the scent that was hers alone before his lips closed over mouth. It took him a moment to realize she hadn't returned his kiss.

When he raised his head, he didn't know whether to be angry or...what. Never had a woman refused him.

"Get off me," she ground out.

He shook his head, not trusting his voice just yet.

"I'll scream."

"If you do, you'll bring the rest of the guards down upon us," he whispered.

Shannon jerked in surprise. He hadn't imagined her response earlier, so what was the problem now? Why didn't she want him?

"There are guards?"

He nodded. "Gabriel is taking care of the four we saw. I hear more moving toward us."

Cole rolled off her, but made sure she stayed lying on the ground. "Don't move," he warned as he reached for his weapons that he had dropped when he tackled her.

Once the small axes were retrieved, he strapped his war axe to his back. They sat in silence for several long moments as the guards combed the areas around them. What felt like an eternity later, the guards finally made their way back towards the castle.

Cole was the first to stand. He was still so disturbed about the kiss that he couldn't look at Shannon. He felt, more than saw, Gabriel walk up beside him.

"Who are you?" she asked.

Gabriel answered for him. "I'm Gabriel. A friend of Cole's."

"How did you know I left?"

Her voice shook slightly. The last thing Cole wanted was for her to fear him, as well. He turned to face her. It was time for honesty.

"Gabriel saw you leave."

Her hands went to her hips as she glared at him. "What, you think because of one kiss that you own me? I don't think so, mister."

Cole blinked, not expecting her angry tone. "What?"

But she wasn't finished. "Why? Why me? Why does everyone want me?"

She was close to hysterics, and apparently Gabriel noticed it as well because his warrior stance disappeared.

"Easy, Shannon," Cole said softly. "There's a reason we came after you. We'll explain everything, but we must return to the tavern."

She shook her head. "I'm not going back. I finally managed to escape, and you want me to return to that hell hole? I don't think so."

Cole had heard her different accent upon first meeting her, but now that she was upset, her natural tone and way of speaking shown through. "Where are you from?"

She folded her arms over her chest. "You wouldn't know it."

"All right," Cole said, willing to try another tactic. "When are you from, because you are obviously not from this time?"

Her jaw dropped, and she backed away from him. "Were you there? Were you with the ones responsible for bringing me here?"

"Nay," Gabriel said, his voice smooth as silk. "We have some...experience with what happened though."

Shannon's gaze swung from Gabriel to Cole. "Do you force people to this time?"

Cole shook his head. "We don't, but we have traveled through time before."

"Several times," Gabriel added.

"Oh, God," Shannon murmured.

She began to wobble, so Cole put his arms around her to steady her.

"What are you?" she asked as she looked up at Cole as if he were something other than human.

And for all he knew, he was.

CHAPTER NINE

"We are warriors who travel through time," Cole finally answered.

She swallowed several times before asking, "Warriors for what?"

"For this realm." Cole didn't think Shannon could handle everything just yet, so he planned to give it to her a little at a time. "We battle creatures and evil that would otherwise destroy villages."

"What does this have to do with me?"

Cole dreaded this question. He glanced at Gabriel, who, it appeared, was going to let him do all the talking.

"We need your help."

She shook her head. "There is nothing that you could say that would make me go back there."

Cole took a deep breath and tried again. "Shannon, how long have you been here?"

"About three weeks."

"How many nights have you seen the castle guards come and get someone from the village like they did tonight?"

Her eyes grew round. "You saw me? You were there?"

"We followed the guards," Gabriel replied.

Her gaze flew to him. "Why didn't you do something to save that poor girl? She's dead now because you warriors didn't do a damn thing."

"Actually, we did," Cole interjected before she could go on. "That girl is with her family now."

Shannon's forehead furrowed in thought. "That's why the guards came to question you?"

Cole nodded. "Please answer my question."

She looked down at the ground and licked her lips. "It started shortly after I came to be here. It's not every night, but nearly, and we never know who they'll take." She raised her gaze to Cole. "Can you stop them?"

"We can, and we will, but that's why we need your help."

She shook her head sadly and wiped at her eyes. "I'm not a brave person. I just want to return to my own time, my own home, and have my life."

"What if we promise you won't be harmed in any way?" Gabriel asked.

She chuckled and rolled her eyes. "How can you promise that?"

Gabriel gave her a knowing smile. "I don't make a promise I can't keep. None of the Shields do."

"Shields," Shannon repeated and looked at Cole. "Is that what you call yourselves?"

"Aye. And we are very good at what we do."

She sighed as if debating with herself, and Cole gave her a few moments before he continued.

"Shannon, if you go back to the tavern, then you can help me and Gabriel discover just what is going on at the castle. The people are being taken there, but we don't know why."

"Haven't you heard the roar?" she asked. "You would have to be deaf not to hear it."

"We've heard it," Gabriel said."

Cole took a step toward Shannon. "What is it?"

She shrugged. "I have no idea, no one does. If I didn't know better, I would say it was some wild animal, a very large wild animal. But, all the years watching animal programs on TV never showed me an animal that made that kind of sound."

"Just where are you from?" Gabriel asked, exasperated.

"The future," she said softly. "A place called America."

Cole's head jerked to Gabriel. That was where Val and Roderick were. "What city?"

Her eyes narrowed on him. "You've heard of it?"

"Aye," he nearly growled. "What city?"

"Chicago."

Gabriel moved closer to Cole. "Is that near Houston?"

"No, quite a ways away actually. Why? And how in the world do you know Houston?"

Cole ran a hand down his face. He had hoped of some news about Val and Roderick, but that was impossible until Aimery appeared. "Two of the Shields are there."

"Oh," she replied softly.

Shannon watched Cole and Gabriel as they stood silently before her. They had gotten so excited when they discovered where she was from that she had hated to disappoint them.

The entire night was like a bad dream, one that she couldn't wake from. They had asked her to do the impossible – return to the tavern. She had to wonder if they knew just what they asked, but by the regret in Cole's dark eyes, she figured he did.

She hadn't lied. She wasn't brave, the exact opposite really. She didn't watch scary movies since she would always have nightmares for days afterwards. She didn't get on thrill rides at amusement parks because she knew she'd be on one when it broke and came crashing to the ground.

The riskiest thing she did was get in her car every day and drive the streets of Chicago. And that was as much risk as she could manage.

"Shannon?"

Cole's deep voice called to her. She knew what he waited for, but wasn't sure she could do it.

"Think of the lives you can save," Gabriel said.

"There are some people, like you two," Shannon said, "that want to be heroes. I don't want to be a hero. I just want to be left alone."

When Cole gripped each of her shoulders, she welcomed his warmth and his strength that seeped through her clothes and into her skin.

"For whatever reason, Fate has picked you. You're a strong woman. You can do this. And Gabriel and I will protect you. I am but one floor above you."

She looked from one warrior to the other. Yes, they were warriors, from their leather clothes to the unique array of weapons they carried.

Men of strength.

Men of cunning.

Men of stealth.

"I never believed men like you actually existed," she said after several attempts to swallow and wet her dry mouth. "I know I'm going to regret this, but all right."

The smile Cole bestowed on her was almost enough to make it worthwhile, and the gratitude shining in Gabriel's eyes gave her confidence the boost it needed.

"Come, we will sneak back in through my chamber," Cole said.

Shannon handed her sack of food to Gabriel. "Here, keep this. You'll need it more than I will now."

He smiled and accepted the gift. "We will always be near."

She gave him a small wave before he disappeared into the forest. She then turned to Cole. "Let's go before I change my mind."

He led her back toward the village, and she made sure to stay right behind him. She eyed the small axes he carried in each hand, not because she was appalled by them, but because of the beautiful craftsmanship that obviously went into them.

Even in the moonlight she could see the intricate design on the handles, and she would guess that the rings around the two-foot handles weren't brass but real gold.

And the blades themselves, they were magnificent. From tip to tip they were about ten inches in length, with a large curve to the blade. The edge of the blade had the same intricate knot work on it as well, lending an almost ethereal feel to the weapons.

She was so busy admiring the weapons that she never saw Cole stop. She ran into the back of him, but he spun around and caught her before she could stumble backwards.

"Sorry," she said breathlessly as she gazed into his velvety brown eyes.

"Are you all right?"

She nodded. "I just wasn't paying attention. I was admiring your axes."

"Really?" he said as he set her on her feet. "Care to see one?"

She eagerly accepted the weapon. "It's much lighter than I expected," she said as she held it with one hand. After she swung it around a couple of times, she ran a hand down the handle. "It's very beautiful. Where did you get it?"

"A special craftsman made it for me."

"It must have been well worth the coin it cost you," she said as she handed him back the axe.

He hooked the axe through his belt and smiled at her. "Anything this beautiful and valuable is worth the cost."

They stared at each other for what seemed like an eternity before Cole held out his hand.

"Ready?"

"No," Shannon said as she placed her hand inside

his large, warm one. She knew what awaited her, but she was trusting Gabriel and Cole to keep their word and keep her alive. She just prayed they did.

"All will be fine. I'll watch you to make sure no harm comes to you. I give you my word."

"And I'll hold you to it," she whispered as they ran from the safety of the forest toward the tavern.

They reached the building just as they heard someone coming toward them. Cole flattened her against the building and moved so that he stood facing her.

"Trust me," he said just before his mouth captured her lips.

Shannon nearly melted on the spot. His kisses were as satisfying as only Heaven could be, and as intoxicating as the sweetest wine. It had taken everything she had in the forest to push him away, and she wasn't about to do it again.

As his tongue glided skillfully into her mouth, she sighed and softened against him, drinking in his scent, his sexuality. There was something about Cole that made her crave to feel him inside her, ache to feel his hands on her body.

Her breasts tightened and tingled as he molded her against his hard chest. She couldn't stop her hands from slowly roaming up his bulging chest to his massive shoulders and his thick neck.

Everything around her faded to nothing.

She forgot where she was, what she was doing, and why she was there. All her mind and body wanted was Cole.

To her disappointment, he ended the kiss.

Shannon's chest rose and fell as if she had run a marathon. Her hands shook, and her knees trembled as she tried to examine what Cole did to her.

"Oh, God," she murmured and closed her eyes as Cole leaned his forehead against hers.

He stayed silent, and after a moment she realized why. Castle guards walked all around them inspecting the area.

"We'll never get back in," she whispered.

His answer was a smile and a wink.

It was just a moment later that the guards walked away. Cole leaned away from her and gripped her waist.

"Are you ready?"

"No," she answered as he picked her up and lifted over his head. Her fingers gripped the edge of his window sill, and with the help of his hands holding her feet, she was able to get a better hold and then move her feet against the stones to give herself some leverage. She never realized how much the rock climbing lessons she took would come in handy.

She pulled herself up and through the window to land in a heap on the floor. Before she could roll over and get to her feet, Cole stood over her and helped her up.

"Now what?" she asked.

"We get you to your chamber."

To her great shame, she nearly asked him if she could stay in his. Not because she was afraid, but because there was a bed and she wanted him in it, making love to her.

Hard, fast, soft, slow, she didn't care as long as his

hands and mouth were touching her.

She shook her head and tried to tell her body to calm down, but it refused to listen as her sex clenched, and when Cole walked past her, rubbing against her arm, she nearly reached out for him.

"Are you all right?"

She raised her gaze to his and managed a nod. He stared at her a moment before taking her hand and leading her to the door. Shannon took one last look at his bed as they slipped into the hallway.

"Stay here," Cole mouthed as he slowly walked down the stairs.

Shannon watched him, intrigued by his stealth. He held an axe in each hand now, prepared for anything that might come his way. When he reached the bottom and found no one, he motioned her down.

She walked the stairs as quickly and quietly as she could. Fear raced up her spine as if at any moment they would be caught, and though she knew Cole to be a fine warrior, he couldn't help them alone, not against the castle guards and the Baron.

When her feet finally touched the floor, she fairly raced to her room. Just as she was about to open the door, Cole jerked her to a stop. She let him pull her against his chest, loving the feel of him against her.

"Remember, Shannon, we will protect you," he whispered in her ear before he gave her a quick kiss on the lips.

And then he was gone.

For several minutes, Shannon stood outside her room. She waited for Cole to return to his room, and after she heard his door close, she turned to hers and entered her room.

She didn't even attempt to change her clothes, but fell across the bed fully clothed. The night had not ended with her escaping Benton as she had wanted, but she had to wonder if she wasn't where she really wanted to be.

With Cole.

CHAPTER TEN

Cole sat with his head in his hands as the sun crested the horizon. He had gotten little sleep, and when his dreams hadn't been filled with Shannon dying in his arms, he dreamed of making love to her. He woke in such a state of arousal that he was in physical pain, with a dark mood to match.

He knew convincing Shannon to return had been the right thing to do, but after another night of the nightmares, he was now questioning himself.

Had he done the right thing?

Could he and Gabriel really keep her safe, just the two of them? If all the Shields were together, he wouldn't doubt it for a moment. He was too close to this situation, and he found he didn't like it one bit.

Several times last night he found himself about to leave his room to check on Shannon, and had to make himself return to his bed and lie down. No woman had ever managed to get under his skin the way she had, and he blamed it on the vivid dreams of her death.

It was the only explanation.

When he heard movement downstairs, he rose from the bed and walked to his bowl of water on the small table. He quickly washed and shaved a day's growth of beard, and changed clothes before he went for his breakfast.

He had to force himself not to look for Shannon. As he took his usual seat in the back corner, he let his gaze rove over the small room, noting every detail.

Only the customers renting a room were in the tavern this early in the morning, but Cole knew it would only be a matter of moments before the townsfolk began to fill the tables.

The smell that was all Shannon's reached him, and he found himself both eager to look at her and fearful of what he would see in her eyes. Would she hate him for convincing her to return? Would he repulse her for using her as he had? Or would there be a welcoming smile?

He slowly moved his gaze to her face and saw her downcast eyes. He clenched his jaw, wishing he hadn't done what he had, wishing he had allowed her to leave when she had had the chance instead of risking her life as she was now doing.

Then he saw the fresh wound near her hairline above her right eye and rage engulfed him. He knew who had dared to touch her.

Again.

And this time Benton would pay.

"No," she whispered as she set his plate of food before him. "Leave it, Cole. Don't give him reason to seek you out again."

Cole was about to argue with her when her gaze met his. In her eyes, he saw the fear she wasn't able to hide, and he vowed then and there, that before he left the village, something would be done about Benton.

"Remember your promise. You can't keep it if you're dead."

Her words jerked him out of his rage. She was right. He had to keep a level head. Slowly, Cole lowered his gaze to stare mindlessly at his food.

When did Shannon become so important? Sure, he enjoyed his share of women, and he protected them when necessary. Yet, the feelings assaulting him now weren't the normal protectiveness he felt towards other women. It was something more, much more.

And it scared the hell out of him.

The urge, the need to wrap his hands around Benton's neck and squeeze until all breath left his lungs was almost too much to bear, but bear it he would.

Too much was at stake – namely, the salvation of the realm of Earth and the Fae realm.

So, with an ironclad will, he lifted a bite of the food into his mouth. He never tasted it. His mind was on discovering just what kind of creature they were up against.

There was no need to search for the wielder of the blue stone, the stone that summoned and controlled the creature. The wielder was the baron.

Finding the stone, however, was something else entirely.

Cole wasn't afraid to face the baron, the creature, or any number of men because he was immortal. But Gabriel was another matter. No one, not even Gabriel, knew if he was mortal or not, or from where he hailed.

The Shields had already lost one. Cole didn't wish to report back to Hugh and inform him that Gabriel had also been lost.

Somehow, someway, he and Gabriel must do this alone. Two against an army and a creature so evil he had been trapped in another realm. Not bad odds considering what type of warriors he and Gabriel were.

Cole leaned back in his chair and crossed his arms over his chest. He was a warrior, a man who had a gift for fighting.

Maybe it was time for more of it.

Aimery ran a hand down his weary face. For centuries, the Fae had thought they had guarded their realm and Earth against the evil that penetrated other realms, yet it seemed they had been wrong.

Woefully wrong.

The Shields had been his idea, the gathering of the finest warriors throughout time and history, warriors so great that they lived on in legends.

Now, there were only five Shields left. Five men out of nearly a hundred he knew would give their lives to save his realm and Earth. Five of the finest warriors that had ever breathed.

And he had separated them.

Together they were invincible. Apart...apart they were dangerous, but would it be enough?

Aimery hung his head as he wondered over and over again if he had made the correct decision.

Aimery.

The call from his king brought him to his feet. He immediately walked from his office at the palace to the throne room. Floors of gilded blue stone that was only found on the Fae realm sparkled beneath his feet. Murals of their history from the beginning through great wars until present day lined the walls of the long hall toward the throne room, yet Aimery didn't see them.

His mind was still on his Shields.

Bright light showed all around him as he stepped in front of the king's and queen's thrones. The great dome roof above him allowed the light to shine through, day or night.

Aimery went down on his knee, wondering why he had been summoned.

"Is everything all right?"

His queen's soft, melodic voice brought his head up. Her Fae blue eyes shown with concern as she watched him, and Aimery knew lying wasn't an option.

"I'm not sure, my queen," he answered.

King Theron bade Aimery to rise. "What do you mean?"

Aimery looked from Theron to Rufina. "I did the unthinkable."

"You are the Fae commander. What could you have possibly done that you think is that awful?" Rufina asked with a smile.

Aimery swallowed and clasped his hands behind him. "I separated the Shields."

Silence echoed around him until Theron gained his feet and walked to stand in front of him.

"I have no doubt in my mind that you split the Shields up for a very important reason, my friend."

The weight of Aimery's guilt increased with his king's words. "I knew separating them would limit their chances of survival."

"Then tell us the reason you chose to do it," Rufina said softly.

Aimery sighed and paced in front of them. "Reports of more creatures come daily, and with the search for the other four girls...."

"Girls?" Rufina repeated.

Aimery stopped and looked at her, but before he could speak, Theron did.

"Don't you remember, my love? Aimery and I found the ancient text of the other realm. They were about to be destroyed and they sent out twelve of their young to Earth?"

Rufina nodded. "Ah, yes. Six boys and six girls. That's, right," she said. "You found one. Hugh's mate."

"Aye," Aimery said. "All six boys are dead. They never survived their times. War took most of them, but a duel took the last. One of the girls was taken in a plague."

"Which leaves only five," Theron finished. "The question is, will the five be able to break the evil?"

"Do they even know how?" Rufina asked.

Aimery shrugged. "Mina, Hugh's mate, recalls nothing. I'm confident that once all five are gathered together they'll be able to decipher what they need to do."

Theron regarded him closely. "What is it you are

keeping from us?"

Aimery sighed. "Not only are the women scattered throughout time and the entire breadth of Earth, but they know of them now."

"They?" Theron asked breathlessly. "Tell me you aren't referring to the evil that threatens us.

Slowly, Aimery nodded. "Between the creatures and searching for the girls, the Shields had to be split. Our time is growing short."

Theron slammed his fist into his hand. "If only the devils would dare to attack here, then we could fight them."

"That's the point, my darling," Rufina said, her eyes raised to the beautiful dome ceiling. "They know they cannot defeat us in our realm. They must reach us through Earth."

Aimery nodded. "As it is, we are nearly overstepping the boundaries by arming the Shields and shifting them through time."

"Yet we will continue," Theron said stiffly. "We have no other choice."

Aimery watched as Rufina rose and walked into her husband's arms. The Fae and Earth had battled evil to continue on once already, but this time, the evil was greater, more powerful – and everywhere.

Aimery turned on his heel and left the couple alone. Already the Fae army was stretched thin, but he would send out more of his men to look for the women.

The Shields were doing all they could do. He needed to arm them with as much information as he could.

CHAPTER ELEVEN

Shannon's head ached as if twelve dozen marching bands played inside her mind. Her vision was blurred, and she feared she had a concussion.

It was nearly as bad as when she had been hurled into her current place, though, at the time, she hadn't realized she had been traveling through time.

If only she hadn't walked into her room without checking to see if Benton had returned, for he had been waiting for her.

As soon as she had thrown herself on her bed to try and manage some rest, he had yanked her off it by her hair. Her instinct had been to cry out, but she feared Cole might hear her. As much as she wanted him to save the day, he had a village to save.

Besides, she knew Benton wouldn't kill her. Not yet.

"Tell me why you weren't in bed," he had demanded, his nose practically pressed against hers.

She tried to jerk out of his grasp, which only

managed to anger him more. "I heard the guards and went to see what was going on."

"You know better," he ground out. "I told you to stay inside your chamber at all times, no matter what you hear or see."

The anger blazing in his black eyes frightened her. If he knew what she had seen that night, and that she had nearly escaped, she had no doubts he would kill her on the spot.

He shoved her away from him. Unprepared to be thrown off balance, Shannon fought to keep her footing. Her hand found the bedpost just as she began to fall. She righted herself and turned toward Benton. The rage that had overtaken him still had him in its hold. She knew then she wouldn't come out of their altercation without some kind of wound.

"I told him to keep you locked in the dungeon," he said as he stepped toward her. "He wouldn't listen to me. Said he had enough to worry about."

"Who?" she asked, her voice shaky with fear.

Benton laughed evilly. "You know who, don't try to play coy with me."

"The baron?"

Benton nodded and took another step toward her. "You aren't nearly worth the coin he pays me to keep you here."

Before Shannon could register that he had raised his meaty fist, it came flying at her. Her teeth rattled as her head swung around and her feet came off the ground from the force of the hit.

The real pain came as she started to fall and hit her head on the edge of the bedpost. Pain lanced its way through her body, but she knew more was to come and quickly curled up in a ball.

There was a loud thud as something heavy hit the floor.

Dimly, she heard something move in her room. Slowly, so as not to cause herself more pain, she moved her head and saw the outline of a man standing over what appeared to be Benton lying on the floor.

"Shannon?"

Her eyes misted with tears at Gabriel's voice. "Yes," she managed to squeak.

As she started to sit up, Gabriel was there beside her, his hands on her arms. "Don't," he warned. "You need to lie still for a moment."

She watched him pull out a black velvet bag that he laid on the floor, untied, and then opened. Inside was an array of dried herbs, flowers, and God only knew what else.

There were also tiny vials of liquids, crushed things, and whole things.

"What are you doing?" she asked, now unable to move her cheek from Benton's hit.

"Helping you," he said as he lifted one vial, measured a bit of it into a small bowl, then reached for a dried flower, and began to mix them.

"Benton," she started, but he quickly silenced her with a look.

"He won't remember being hit in the morning. That I promise you."

The pain was nearly too much for her now. She wasn't the type of person to reach for any kind of pain medicines, but right about now she wished for something just so she could blink without throbbing in pain.

A coolness met her cheek, and she opened her eyes to see Gabriel spreading something on her face.

"It will fade the bruise and heal it by morning. How is your head?"

"Hurting," she ground out, not wanting him to see just how much pain she was in.

"That I won't be able to heal overnight, but I'll be able to help with the pain and begin the healing quicker."

Shannon no longer cared if he sewed a rabbit to her head. The ache had spread everywhere. Even her hair hurt now.

"Shannon?"

She heard Gabriel calling to her as if from a great distance, but she couldn't answer him. Then she stopped trying altogether. The darkness was much better than the hell she lived in.

The next thing she knew, she woke to find the sun just coming up over the horizon and Benton banging on her door. True to Gabriel's word, Benton didn't remember a thing after her beating.

Shannon set the empty ale mugs down and walked to the kitchen. On her way, she walked by a mirror. No bruise marked her face, and the cut on her forehead was small compared to what she knew it must have looked like last night. She owed Gabriel a thank you.

In the back of her mind, she wondered what Cole would have done had he seen Benton beating her. That first night, he hadn't known her, yet he had stopped him from hitting her. And just now, once he had seen her cut, the fury that had blazed in his beautiful chocolate eyes had sent a thrill through her.

Cole was the type of man to stop anyone from hitting a woman. And though she knew she wasn't special to him, she allowed herself to believe it for just a moment.

Benton yelling her name brought her back to reality. By the time she reentered the dining room, Cole was gone. She hated that she missed him, a man she barely knew but a man that held her spellbound with his sensual smile and body that exuded sexuality nonetheless.

And his kisses. She couldn't even think about them without feeling moisture between her legs.

While she wondered again how she could have managed to allow Cole to talk her into returning to the tavern as she placed plates of food in front of a table of men, their conversation caught her attention.

"She got away," one of them mumbled. "First time that has happened."

"Aye," another added. "She told her family that it was two men who killed the guards and freed her."

Another snorted. "Two men. I doubt that. 'Twould take twice that amount to take out twelve of the castle guards."

"Still, I'd like to meet these men."

"Who do you think it is?" the one Shannon served asked.

She tried to see his face, but wasn't able to see anything other than a big, bushy salt and pepper beard.

"I wish I knew," someone said.

"They'll come again tonight. The beast will need to

be fed twice after what happened last eve."

Shannon couldn't help but shudder at the man's words. He was most likely correct. She itched to find Cole and give him what little news she had.

She tried to ignore the fact that she wanted to give him much more than news.

Cole drummed his fingers on the trunk of the massive ash tree as he stared at the castle. Usually, castles hummed with activity from the village and within, yet this...castle...wasn't the usual.

A creature of pure evil dwelled within, and the person responsible for its appearance was hidden inside, as well.

"Not for long," Cole mumbled as he watched the guards change at the gatehouse tower.

His gaze moved to the six other towers as the guards changed there, as well. The towers were entirely too tall to climb, and the round shape would make it doubly hard.

His and Gabriel's disguise as monks might be able to work again, but just in case they needed another route, Cole was going to find it this day.

He leisurely walked through the forest until he reached the castle, then he strolled around the castle. It was heavily defended, the walls thick, the towers high, and the guards plenty. But every fortress had a weak spot.

The forest surrounded the village and the back half of the castle. The castle was built on a rocky incline that gave it an added advantage to any army trying to attack.

It was at the back of the castle, in the dense forest, that Cole stumbled upon a stone wall that protruded from the castle into the forest. Curious, Cole followed the wall through the forest until it connected once again to the castle.

As he contemplated just what was inside the wall, the roar of the creature sounded. Cole jerked. The creature was near, very near.

Immediately, Cole began to climb the wall. He had gotten half way up when he heard movement behind him. A quick glance showed the red tunics of the castle guards. With a curse, Cole dropped to the ground and quickly hid.

Cole watched from his hiding spot just a few feet from the wall as the baron and his men walked up.

"Are you sure?" the baron turned and asked one of the guards.

"Aye, my lord. He had dark brown hair, and he was trying to scale the wall."

Gyles narrowed his eyes on the guard. "If there was someone here, he's still in the forest. Find him!" he bellowed.

The guards hastily fanned out into the trees. All but one.

Cole watched as Gyles and the man spoke in hushed tones, and though he tried to catch something of their conversation, he heard nothing.

Gyles turned and walked back to the castle, but the guard stayed and looked into the trees as if he could see through them and find Cole.

Cole looked the man over. He stood well over six feet, and his massive frame could crush a man's skull. This one Cole and Gabriel would have to watch out for.

He waited until the huge guard turned and left, then Cole crawled from the thick underbrush near the castle wall and stood. He glanced at the wall and thought of trying again to climb over, but the sound of the guards thrashing in the forest quickly changed his mind.

Cole found Gabriel at the back of the tavern watching Shannon. "How is she?"

Gabriel regarded him a moment. "She's fine."

"What happened last eve?"

Gabriel pushed away from the tree he leaned against and ran his hands down his prized bow. "As soon as I saw what was going on, I intervened. I told you I would protect her when you couldn't."

"She got hurt.

"And I treated that as well."

Cole sighed and turned away. "Thank you."

"Tell me, my brother. Why does she mean so much to you?"

"I wish I knew," Cole answered softly.

They sat in silence watching Shannon through the open windows for a time. Cole didn't know where the protectiveness for Shannon had come from. He protected all women and children, but with Shannon, it was different.

He told himself it was because she had been brought here without her consent, but he knew it was much more than that. He just didn't want to dig and find out the truth. Not yet.

"There's a wall in the back of the castle," he said to take his mind off of Shannon.

Gabriel glanced at him. "Where does it lead?"

"Into the forest, then back around to the castle. From what I can tell, it makes a large circle."

"Odd, don't you think?"

"Very. I heard the creature within and tried to climb the wall but wasn't able to get in before the guards came. There's a man we need to keep an eye out for."

"Really?" Gabriel asked, his interest peaked. "And who is this man?"

Cole turned to look at Gabriel. "You'll recognize him on sight. He has to be the largest man I've ever seen."

"Hmmm," Gabriel said. "I'm looking forward to meeting him. We've done enough watching and listening. I'm ready for battle."

CHAPTER TWELVE

As soon as Shannon spotted Cole, she wanted to run to him and share everything she had learned that day, which was more than she expected.

Knowing she needed an excuse to go to him, she brought him a mug of ale, trying to make it appear as though she wasn't in a hurry.

It had helped her to know that all during the day, Cole had been there, watching her, protecting her. Oh, she knew Cole and Gabriel changed positions so Cole could gather a look around, but she liked to delude herself into thinking it was only Cole watching her.

She leaned as close as she could to Cole as she sat the mug next to him. "I have information for you."

"How are you feeling?"

She blinked, not thinking she heard him correctly.

"Does your head ache?" he asked.

"No," she whispered. The happiness that swam through her body at knowing he had been worried about her was intense.

"Meet me in my chamber after midnight," he said just before she straightened.

Joy leapt in her heart until she realized they weren't meeting to make out, but so that she could give him the information.

What is wrong with me? I'm acting like a man thinking of sex all the time.

She blamed it on Cole. Men like him shouldn't exist. He kept her mind jumbled and her body in constant need. But she would have to remember he wasn't for her.

Her eyes met his, and for a moment, she saw his desire. It was blatant, as if he wanted her to see it.

She was quickly becoming a wanton, something she had never imagined herself to be, and with a man she hardly knew.

Aimery had called a gathering of his generals. In order for the Fae to stay ahead of this game the evil played, he needed to give his generals as much knowledge as he could.

"Any news from your scouts," he asked them.

Michyl rose. "My scouts sense the evil, but have found nothing they can fight. The evil seems to know our next move before we make it."

Aimery thought over Michyl's words. If it was true, it meant either the evil was able to read their thoughts, or they had a traitor. And neither option was good.

"My men are watching over Stone Crest," Sebastian said as he stood. "No evil has ventured there since the gargoyle, but if the Chosen are to be held there, I'll need more men."

"Then more you'll have," Aimery said. "Dom, how go your scholars on discovering where the creatures are trapped?"

Dom slowly shook his head. "We've searched many realms, Aimery, but have found nothing yet."

Aimery fisted his hands. He had hoped by now they would have more information. "We have a long road ahead of us, men. If the evil is too cowardly to fight us on our own realm, we need to keep the Shields armed and ready to battle when needed. Any information, no matter how trivial you think it might be, needs to be brought to me. It was that trivial information that led us to discover the Chosen ones."

He waited until they left his office before he put his head in his hands and sighed. How he longed to find out who the evil was and end this.

Shannon thought the night would never come. The anticipation of meeting Cole had helped to make the evening pass, but once she was in her bed, all she could think about was seeing Cole.

She could well imagine the seconds that ticked by as she waited. Without her watch, she had no idea when it was midnight, but she stayed as long as she could before creeping out of her room and up the stairs.

Just as she had expected, Benton left a few hours after the inn had closed for the night. It was the only reason Shannon felt safe enough to leave her room, that and because she knew Gabriel watched her.

She raised her hand to lightly knock on Cole's door when it was suddenly thrown open and he jerked her inside.

"About time," he murmured, as he looked first one way down the hall and then the other before closing and barring the door.

"I didn't know what time it was." Just being in the room with him sent her body into overload. She crossed her arms over her chest to try and hide her nipples, which had gone hard as soon as she touched him.

The heat of him, the delicious manly scent of him, and the sexuality that fairly poured off of him had her body aquiver. She shivered, not from the cool night air, but in expectation of what she wished would come.

He took a step toward her until their bodies nearly brushed. "Do you hurt?" he asked as his hand gently touched her forehead.

"Only a little. Whatever Gabriel gave me helped."

"I'm sorry."

She looked into his eyes, made even darker by the glow of the lone candle by the bed. "For what?"

"I should have looked in your chamber before you went inside."

She quickly covered his mouth with her hand. The heat of his breath as his lips opened made her weak in the knees. "Don't," she said after a deep breath. "I'm fine."

His gaze searched hers for a moment until he was satisfied with whatever he saw. He lightly kissed her fingers, then gently moved her hand from his mouth.

"What did you hear?"

She smiled then as she recalled what she had heard. "So very much."

"Tell me," he urged as he moved her to the table near the hearth.

She sank into a chair and licked her lips. "The townspeople know of the creature."

"Really?" he asked and sat.

She nodded. "They said as much, but from what I gather, no one has seen it. It doesn't come to the village. Instead, the guards come at night and pick a person randomly."

"I don't think it's random," Cole said as he leaned back.

"Why? The baron rarely comes to the village, and never lets anyone inside the castle gates."

Cole tapped a finger on the table. "The baron may not come into the village, but he has people like Benton that gather information for him."

"True."

"And didn't you tell us last night that Benton had left the tavern?"

She nodded. "He left again tonight. He must be going to the castle to give Gyles updates."

"On you?" Cole asked.

"Could be. Benton made mention that Gyles was paying him to keep me at the tavern."

Cole leaned forward. "Do you know what they have planned for you?"

"No. I've asked several times, but no one will tell me."

"What about how the villagers are picked for the creature? Is it just young people?"

She shook her head. "Several older ones have been taken. Men, women, young or old. It doesn't matter. I have noticed that they haven't taken children."

"I don't think they will. Apparently the creature has a large appetite."

Shannon looked away and tried to swallow as she realized Cole was saying the children wouldn't be enough of a meal.

"I apologize," he said.

"No," she said and looked back at him. "You were only stating a fact, despite how gruesome I might think it is."

"Did you hear anything else?"

"Everyone knows of you and Gabriel."

When Cole frowned, she quickly amended her story. "They know that two men stopped the castle guards, but they don't know exactly who. The village is abuzz with it."

"I was hoping the girl didn't see us."

"Apparently she did. She was quick to tell her family about it, and they hastily spread the word."

"Damnation."

"That's not all. Apparently, whatever the creature is will desire two the next time."

"When is the next time?" Cole asked as he sat up straighter.

Shannon shrugged. "I have no idea. They thought maybe tonight, but if that's the case, the guards would have already been to town."

"Exactly. Which means they'll come tomorrow

night."

She nodded, not wanting to think of that just yet. "The family of the girl that was taken last night tried to leave the village today."

"What happened to them?"

"They were taken to the castle," she whispered.

Cole nodded and sighed. "Which explains why they didn't come for anyone tonight."

Shannon hadn't considered that. She lowered her gaze and thought about the family that would die this night. "I suppose."

Cole's large hand covered hers, and she raised her gaze to him. "Gabriel and I gave you a promise. You'll be safe."

"I know."

Suddenly, Cole drew in a ragged breath and rose to his feet to pace near the window. "Anything else?" he asked.

"There is a man, a guard that Gyles keeps with him at all times. He's a giant of a man, rarely comes into town, but the people were speaking of him today. If you see him, run and don't look back. He'll kill you. That's what he does for Gyles."

Shannon watched as Cole spun around, a small smile on his face. "I saw the man you speak of. He is a large brute."

"You aren't afraid?"

He chuckled. "You can't face what I do every day and fear a mere man."

He had a point.

"Do you know what is behind the castle?" Cole asked.

"Behind the castle? No. I've never been to the castle."

"Has anyone spoken of it?"

She thought back over her time at the inn and shook her head. "I don't think so. What is it?"

"I'm not sure. It's a stone wall and makes a large circle in the forest."

"Is that were the creature is?"

Cole shrugged and took a step toward her. Her pulse doubled at the look in his eye, the look of need. She sat clutching the table until he reached her. His hands tugged her from her seat to stand before him.

"You shouldn't have returned here," he said.

"You asked me to."

"I know."

His hands ran over her arms, to her shoulders, neck, and into her hair. She had forgotten she had taken down her hair until his hands plunged into its thickness. Her eyes closed, and she reveled in the feel of his hands on her scalp and neck.

"Ye gods, you are beautiful," he whispered as he lowered his head.

Shannon watched him through half closed lids, silently begging for his kiss.

"Tell me you don't want my kiss," he demanded softly.

"I don't want your kiss."

His husky voice poured over her like honey. "I don't believe you."

"That's because I lied."

Cole knew he should send her on her way, forget the passion he felt for her, because if they kissed, if he tasted her sweet lips again, he wouldn't be able to stop there.

Yet, knowing what he should do and actually doing it proved impossible. He flexed his fingers in her thick, glossy brunette mane and drew her toward him. Her lips were parted, as if she waited for him, needed him as much as he needed her.

Cole tried one last time to make himself release her, but his body simply refused to listen to his brain. And before he could think more on it, he lowered his mouth and took her lips in a kiss meant to intoxicate her and brand her to him.

He smiled inwardly as her fingers dug into his shoulders and a half sigh, half moan broke from between her precious lips as he moved his mouth to her jaw and down her neck.

Her skin, softer than the finest Fae garments, responded to his touch as though she had been made for him. And his body ignited. He returned to her lips and their siren call, plunging his tongue into her mouth and tasting all of her, conquering her.

He couldn't get enough. Her kisses only made him want more, and the feel of her soft hands on his body had him yearning for her touch--skin against skin, body against body.

With extraordinary effort, he managed to pull away. He looked down at her beautiful face with her swollen lips and eyes burning with desire. He held himself back by a thin thread that at any moment would break, but he had to give her one last chance.

"Shannon," he said between great gulps of air. "I'm going to lay you on my bed and make love to you all night unless you leave this chamber right now."

She wrapped her arms around his neck and rose up to kiss him, but he stopped her.

"Last chance," he warned.

Her honey brown eyes stared deep into his. "I want this. I want you."

Cole let loose the breath he had held as he closed his eyes in relief. Women didn't turn him away, and this was the first time he had been afraid that one might. He had said he would let her go, but in truth, he wasn't sure he would have been able.

Thankfully, now he wouldn't have to find out.

He opened his eyes and saw her small smile as she watched him. With a groan, Cole bent and picked her up. She instinctively wrapped her legs around his waist with her skirts bunching between them.

Cole walked to the bed and lay down atop Shannon. His body sizzled with unbridled lust and a need that had to be fed. With his hands on either side of her head, he rose up and gazed down at her.

She was an incredible sight with her dark hair fanned out around her like a crown, and her breasts rising and falling rapidly as she ran her hands over his chest.

Cole leaned back on his knees and began to remove his vest and tunic. Her hands eagerly joined him as she sat up and helped him remove his clothes. When he sat bare-chested before her, she sighed and ran her hands over him as if he was some prized silk.

He leaned his head back and relished in the feel of her hands as they discovered him. Her touch was soft, sensuous, and damn near torture. He bunched the covers in his hands to keep from touching her, but it was fast becoming impossible.

When her delightful lips met his skin, he jerked and found himself shaking with the need to have a taste of her, to learn her as she was learning him.

Her lips, as soft as her hands, kissed and licked his neck, shoulders, abdomen, and chest, and with each heartbeat it became clearer to Cole that Shannon was different from the others. His body had known that upon first seeing her.

He allowed her to kiss and touch him until he burned with need so bright nothing shone but Shannon. He quickly captured her hands and found her lips in a fiery kiss.

"My turn," he whispered as he began to unlace her gown.

It didn't take them long to shed her clothes, leaving her bare except for a blood red lace garment that covered her breasts and the apex of her thighs.

He reached out and gently touched the lace, amazed at the soft feel of it and how it cupped her breasts to mold them perfectly.

She smiled up at him. "It's my bra."

"Your what?"

This time she giggled. "My bra. It helps to hold my breasts."

"Lucky piece of lace," he murmured then looked down at the piece holding her sex. "And this?" he asked as he ran his finger against the lace over her hip.

"My...my panties," she said, her eyes closed as if she savored his touch.

"I envy both pieces," he said as he leaned toward

her and kissed her. "Take off the...bra."

Cole noticed her hands trembling, and he wondered if it was because she was frightened or because of her need. He watched, amazed as she unhooked the garment at her back and it fell away to reveal two perfect breasts made to fit exactly into his hands.

Her creamy breasts rose and fell rapidly, and as he watched, her nipples hardened beneath his gaze.

Shannon was drowning in need. As her breasts tightened and tingled and her nipples became hard as stone, all she could think about was Cole kissing her again.

Just as she was about to start begging, he pulled her against him and gave her another kiss that scorched her to her toes. The man was a born kisser, the kind of man every woman hoped to encounter once in their lives that would give them a kiss that tasted like...paradise.

Cole not only gave her paradise, but he touched her deep within, almost as if her soul had awakened. All with a simple kiss.

Dear lord, what will he do to me when he makes love to me?

Shannon had never feared something so much, nor wanted something so much as she did Cole. He made her feel like a woman, something she never thought she would feel.

As his hands roamed over her back to her butt, she moved her head to the side so he could kiss down the column of her throat, his hot breath and wicked tongue daring her to hold nothing back.

The candle flickered light on the ceiling, bathing

them in its warm golden glow, and Shannon knew that this moment would forever be etched in her memory.

When Cole pulled her to her knees, she quickly followed, her gaze soaking in his astounding abdomen that could surely be used for a washboard. And his chest rippled with deep muscles, muscles that she itched to feel beneath her hands yet again.

The erotic feel of her breasts against his chest left an ache between her legs that made her lightheaded. She moved her hands over his wide shoulders to his thick neck to entwine her fingers in the locks of his silky hair.

Not a single scar marred his body, not even the injury to his shoulder that he had sustained but a few days before. She wasn't given time to think on that as Cole took her in another dazzling kiss.

She held her breath as his hands moved to her waist, then higher until his thumbs grazed the underside of her breasts. She gasped and silently begged for more. Her body was in control and she gave in to it, letting herself explore Cole and herself.

When his hands cupped her breasts and his fingers skimmed over her nipples, she tore her mouth from his and cried out from the pleasure that ripped through her. Her body shook and her sex clenched as he rolled her nipples between his fingers.

The pleasurable pain became too much to bear, and Shannon moved her hips and rubbed against his leg.

"By the gods," she heard Cole murmur as he moved until she was lying back on the bed and he sat between her legs.

Small tremors racked her body as she watched,

waited to see what he would do to her next. He had barely touched her and her body had responded lightening quick. Now, she ached to have him touch her again as her need grew with each second that passed.

"Cole," she whispered, not knowing what to say.

His hand moved to her lips. "Shh. It'll be all right."

No sooner had the words left his mouth than his hands were again on her breasts. She sighed as he kneaded them, letting his palms scrape her sensitive nipples, which ached for his mouth.

When he captured a turgid peak between two fingers and lightly squeezed as his fingers skimmed over the lace of her panties that covered her, her back arched in abandon as she clutched the sheets, helpless to the sensations rocking through her.

Again and again, Cole ran his fingers over the lace, teasing her until she throbbed and her panties were soaked with her arousal.

Finally, she felt the bed shift and opened her eyes to see him remove his pants. As he sprang free, she couldn't help but stare at his cock. He was thick and hard, and all Shannon could think about was having him fill her and ease the ache inside her.

She heard herself panting as he moved toward her. Words had abandoned her, but he seemed to know what she wanted as his thumb moved between her and the band of her panties.

Slowly, he pulled her panties down, exposing her flesh inch by inch. When she was fully exposed, she waited breathlessly for him to take her.

But, he had other ideas.

Breath hissed from between her lips as his fingers glided over her heated, wet sex.

Please. Please! Touch me.

As if he heard her silent pleas, Cole's finger slipped inside her.

A cry tore from Shannon's throat. His finger moved within her, bringing relief, but not nearly enough. She needed more.

She needed him.

Yet, he wasn't done with her. With one finger still inside her, he moved his thumb over her clitoris, sending waves upon waves of delight soaring through her. And when his other hand moved up and rolled a nipple between his fingers, she knew true pleasure then.

She felt her climax coming, felt it building with an intensity that she feared would kill her. When he moved another finger inside her, Shannon jerked as her orgasm erupted, sending millions of tiny lights to go off as she rode the ripples of her climax.

Just as she thought it was over, she felt Cole move and watched as he positioned himself over her. Their eyes met, and the desire burning brightly in his dark depths made her breath catch.

The tip of him entered her and he held still, his eyes closed as if he had just experienced the greatest joy. Then his eyes opened, and he slid his entire length inside her. She gasped at the size of him, but her body quickly accommodated him. A sigh escaped as his fullness surrounded her.

Cole clenched his jaw together as he fought to keep from spilling his seed. He had watched Shannon come alive in his arms, and now, deep inside her, she was tight, wet and oh so hot.

When her legs wrapped around his waist, he closed his eyes and began to move within her. His need drove him onward, pumping faster, harder, until she was panting with him, meeting him thrust for thrust.

His climax could be put off no longer, and just as he was about to give in, he felt her clenching around his cock. With one more thrust, Cole let himself go.

Never had he soared so high or felt so deeply as he did at that moment deep inside Shannon with her arms and legs wrapped tightly around him.

As the last of her tremors rocked her, Cole pulled out of her and rolled to his side

She moved until she faced him, a small smile on her lips. "That was...nothing like I have ever experienced," she said.

"Nor I," he admitted, not realizing until that moment that it was the truth.

She shook her head. "You don't have to say that.…"

"I know," he said, cutting off her words. "I don't say things I don't mean."

She gave him a hesitant smile. "I never cared for sex until now."

Cole found himself chuckling at her until he realized she was serious. "Why?"

She shrugged. "Let's just say that the two other times I had it, it was less than stellar."

"Then I'll endeavor to erase those memories from you," he said as he moved to kiss her.

"You already have."

Her declaration made him want to share something with her. Something he had never told anyone other than the Shields.

A secret that people of this realm wouldn't understand.

CHAPTER THIRTEEN

Cole moved a strand of hair that had fallen in Shannon's face. "I have a secret."

She laughed. "You mean more than being a warrior that kills scary creatures? Not to mention you can travel through time?"

He couldn't help but smile at her words. "Aye, those are big secrets, but I have another."

"Tell me," she urged.

"I'm immortal."

For long moments, she only stared at him. "Truly?" she asked.

"Truly."

"How?"

He shrugged. "Where I come from, it is a normal occurrence."

"And just where is it you hail from?"

"You aren't at all concerned that I'm immortal?" he asked, unable to believe she hadn't run screaming from his chamber.

And maybe, on some level, that's why he had told her, because he knew she was different, what they had just shared was different, and it scared the hell out of him.

She shook her head. "If you can travel through time, why wouldn't you be immortal?"

Cole could only shrug.

"And Gabriel? Is he immortal?"

Cole had completely forgotten about Gabriel. Had he seen them? "We don't know," he finally answered.

"That's odd," Shannon said and snuggled against him. "So, tell me where you come from."

Another secret. Would she be able to handle this one, as well? As it was, he didn't wish to find out. By the time he was ready to give her some reason why she needed to return to her chamber, he looked down and found her asleep.

For the next hour, he watched her drift between dreams until he could hold off no longer. He hurriedly pulled on his clothes then reluctantly woke Shannon to help her dress so she could return to her chamber before Benton returned.

Cole went to his window and found Gabriel in the shadows, after a nod from Gabriel that Shannon's chamber was empty, he walked Shannon to her chamber.

The kiss was supposed to be short and quick, but one taste of her ignited him yet again. He pulled his mouth from hers and opened her door.

"Go," he whispered.

She ran her hand down his face, a satisfied smile on her lips.

"Go on," he urged and closed the door after her.

It wasn't until he returned to his chamber that he realized he'd crossed some line he hadn't known was there.

"Cole."

He turned toward the window and Gabriel.

"Cole?" Gabriel repeated, his brow furrowed. "What have you done?"

Cole shook his head. "The unthinkable."

The next morning, Cole no longer cared about information Shannon could collect for them. He had stayed awake the rest of the night devising a plan, partly because Shannon was a distraction, and partly because he couldn't stand to have another dream that ended with her dying in his arms. As soon as he was able, he found Gabriel.

"I have to get Shannon out of here."

Gabriel took a deep breath and continued to whittle at a piece of wood. "I figured as much. What's your plan?"

"We call Aimery, have him take her back to her time while we get inside the castle and kill the creature and destroy the stone."

"Seems simple enough," Gabriel said sarcastically. He threw down the small piece of wood and sheathed his dagger. "What's gotten into you? You've never let a woman get to you like she has."

"I know," Cole admitted. "I don't know what's happened. I just know that I cannot think straight as long as I know that she's in danger."

"Your dreams," Gabriel stated.

Cole nodded. "The dreams are part of it. I cannot help but feel they are real, and no matter how much we try to keep her safe, we have too much other work to do for just the two of us."

Gabriel pushed away from the tree. "If you let Aimery take her, you'll never see her again."

"I know."

"Then why are you letting her go?"

"It's the only way. She needs to return to her own time."

"All right," Gabriel relented. "Tell me how you expect us to get into the castle."

"Easy," Cole said, a smile pulling at his lips. "I plan on taunting Gyles."

Gabriel wasn't keen on Cole's plan, but he had to admit that it just might work. Cole going in there alone was what Gabriel didn't like. They still had no idea just what creature they were up against, and until they did, Gabriel would rather they stayed together.

Not to mention they hadn't seen the Viking again. What did he have to do with Gyles and the creature, and where was he?

But once Cole made up his mind about something, there was no changing it. Briefly, Gabriel toyed with the idea of calling to Aimery. If anyone could convince Cole to wait it would be the Fae commander, but Gabriel wasn't the kind of man that liked to ask people for help, and in this instance, the situation needed to be dire before he did anything as drastic as call for Aimery.

Gabriel's gaze swung back to the tavern. He kept Shannon within sight at all times. Staying hidden wasn't a problem. The only people in the village that bothered to look at anything were the castle guards, and an entire army could hide from those imbeciles.

He had to admit, Shannon was an attractive woman. She wasn't someone he would have courted, but then again, he didn't court any women. How could a man that couldn't remember his past and not know where he hailed from be able to woo a woman?

Gabriel pulled himself out of his thoughts, for if he lingered too long, the images would start again, and he needed to stay focused. With Cole consumed with Shannon, someone had to watch his back, and that someone was Gabriel.

He had already failed in healing a Shield. He wouldn't be responsible for another's death.

CHAPTER FOURTEEN

Cole stood in the small clearing of the forest and raised his face to the sun as its beams filtered through the branches of the trees. He needed to clear his head, and the only way to do that was to train.

He removed his jerkin and tunic, looked down at the array of axes before him, then reached for the two small single blades. With one in each hand, he twirled them around his head and body, slowly emptying his mind of everything but finding the creature.

Using the techniques the Fae had taught him, he pictured one of the many creatures he had killed and imagined he was fighting it. He lunged, he pivoted, and he attacked the imaginary creature with his axes.

But the smaller blades didn't give him the satisfaction his war axe did. Cole laid the smaller axes aside and palmed the hefty double-headed war axe Aimery had commissioned for him. The axe was a work of art, truly a beautiful piece of weaponry, and it was Cole's favorite. The blade gleamed in the sunlight, and it was easy for him to imagine burying it in the gut of the creature.

Cole used his frustration at not discovering the creature and his confusion about Shannon as his motivation. The training technique quickly took over and he was once more fighting a creature. Except this time, it was the gargoyle that had dared to try and destroy Mina's village, the same gargoyle that had taken Darrick's life.

He swung his axe and ducked, then rolled and came up on his feet as he swung his axe around him. The red eyes of the imaginary gargoyle glowed, and its claws lengthened as it advanced on Cole.

Cole swung his great axe over his head as the gargoyle walked closer, then with a mighty yell, he slammed the war axe into the gargoyle's head.

He blinked as the image of the gargoyle faded. His breath rushed from his lungs and sweat dripped into his eyes, but his body was as quiet as his mind. He laid the axe beside the others and stretched his arms above his head.

He went over his plan once more, making sure there was no chance that Shannon would be hurt in any way. He didn't need Hugh there to tell him he was putting a mortal ahead of the mission, but in order for Cole to do his duty, Shannon had to leave. She consumed him, body, mind, and soul.

No woman had ever done that, and it confused and frightened him. And fear wasn't an emotion Cole felt.

Ever.

He wasn't about to start now.

As he started to reach for his tunic and vest, he

heard movement behind him.

Ever so slightly, he moved his left hand to the dagger in his boot as his right hand reached for the tunic. He palmed the dagger the same time he turned.

And found Benton before him.

"I wondered where you had gone," Benton said as he gazed at the axes. "A fine assortment you have here. Planning to attack anyone?"

Cole fingered the dagger and wondered if he should plant it in Benton's skull. Instead, he said, "Depends. Do you plan on striking Shannon again?"

Benton's lips turned up in a sneer. "She is no concern of yours, and the sooner you realize that, the better off you'll be."

"Says who?"

"Says Gyles. The baron has need of Shannon."

"Why?"

Benton crossed his arms over his barrel chest and regarded him. "You ask many questions for a man who is just visiting our little village. Why the interest in a mere serving wench?"

"I take an interest in all women who find themselves bullied." The more Benton said the more Cole wanted to thrash him.

"Do yourself a favor. Forget her. Forget this place. Leave before Gyles changes his mind."

Now that intrigued Cole. "Changes his mind about what?"

"Allowing you to live."

That's just what Cole needed to hear. "Why should a man who is visiting cause such...disarray...to a mighty baron? Doesn't the baron have many other problems to tend to?"

"Heed my warning," Benton repeated. He glanced down at the axes again before he turned on his heel and strode away.

Cole sheathed the dagger and stared after Benton. *So, the baron is worried about me and what I might do.*

Had anyone seen the smile on Cole's face they would have known death was about to come.

Aimery stood and watched Cole as he poured water over his face from a water skin. The encounter with Benton had been interesting, and most likely something Cole would have omitted telling him.

As Cole pulled his tunic over his head, Aimery made himself visible and walked to him. "I see you've made another friend."

Cole chuckled. "I'm the friendly sort."

"Where is Gabriel?"

Cole hesitated for just a moment, but it was a moment longer than Aimery liked.

Something had happened. Knowing he wouldn't be able to read anything, Aimery still tried to search Cole's mind only to find himself blocked. Gabriel would be the same, so there was no use in that either.

"He's watching over Shannon," Cole finally answered.

Shannon? "Who is this Shannon?"

"The woman brought here from another time."

That got Aimery's attention. He studied Cole's face, noting the teasing glint was gone from his dark brown eyes. "From the future?"

"Aye," Cole answered, eying him.

Aimery closed his eyes and said a silent prayer of thanks. "We need to find Gabriel. I have some information you might need."

Cole nodded, gathered his weapons, and led Aimery to Gabriel who stood in the forest at the back of a tavern, the same building in which Cole was staying.

"Aimery," Gabriel said in surprise, and it seemed, relief.

"Gabriel," he said and clasped the warrior's forearm. "How do things progress?"

"Too damn slowly," Gabriel mumbled. "We've only had two fights."

Aimery couldn't help but smile. "I've seen Val and Roderick."

As he thought, both Cole and Gabriel turned their full attention to him.

"And?" Cole urged.

"They are battling harpies."

Gabriel swore and fisted his hands.

Cole studied Aimery, noting that the Fae had much more to tell them, but was giving it bit by bit. "As in multiple harpies?"

The Fae nodded. "Three to be exact."

"We need to aid them," Gabriel said.

"Nay," Aimery said. "You need to be here."

Cole glanced at Gabriel as his friend ran a hand through his hair in agitation. Cole knew exactly how he felt, for he felt the same. "Are they all right?"

"For now," Aimery said. "We're doing all we can to

figure a way to kill the harpies."

Gabriel touched Cole's shoulder. "If we hurry here, we can help Val and Roderick."

"There's more," Aimery interrupted before Cole could respond.

Cole didn't like the look in Aimery's Fae blue eyes. "What is that?"

"Val and Roderick found another girl with a mark."

Cole blinked, not expecting that at all. "How was she in the same city as the creatures?"

"That is what I wondered," Aimery said as he clasped his hands behind his back. "I then sent more of my army out to scour the realm."

"And?" Gabriel said, his voice edged with anger.

Aimery's gaze met Cole's. "The creatures are there to kill the girl."

Cole felt as if the breath had been kicked from his lungs. "Are you telling me that one of the girls is here, in this very village?"

Aimery nodded.

"By the gods," Cole murmured.

"You need to find the girl," Aimery cautioned. "Keep her away from the creature at all costs. Do you know yet what you battle?"

"Nay," Gabriel answered. "We do know it's in the castle, which means the baron controls it."

"Which also means you should be able to take care of the creature and the stone at once." Aimery shifted his gaze to Cole. "You said Shannon had been brought here from the future. Have you checked her for the mark?"

Cole shook his head. His mind reeled with the new

information.

"Discover if she has the mark this night, Cole. Do what you must, but we need to keep whoever the girl is safe. If they kill one more...."

"We're doomed," Gabriel finished.

Shannon wished she could make the day move faster. Where she used to welcome the night so she could try to escape, she now welcomed it so she could be with Cole.

Cole.

Never in her life had she imagined making love could be so sensual, so erotic, so...wonderful. All she wanted was to spend days, no weeks, in bed with Cole, only rising to eat.

She smiled, laughing inwardly at her fanciful daydreams. A dreamer she wasn't, at least not until Cole. Now, that's all she could find herself doing. Even as she delivered ale and plates of food, she kept thinking of the previous night.

As she returned to the kitchen for more food, she stopped to stretch her legs, which were a little sore from Cole's lovemaking, when she spotted Benton coming towards her.

"You smile overmuch for a woman who wishes not to be here."

Something in his tone told Shannon that she best be careful with her answer. "You asked me to act like a serving wench. I am only doing as I was told."

He leaned close to her and poked her in the

shoulder with his meaty finger. "You don't fool me. I'll find out what has you in such a good humor."

A shudder of fear ran down her back as she watched Benton walk out of the tavern. She knew where he was headed. The castle. But for what purpose? Could her time here be at an end?

Grabbing more mugs of ale, Shannon walked around the dining room, listening for information Cole and Gabriel would need. For somewhere in the back of her mind, she knew something was going to happen tonight.

Cole could stay away from Shannon no longer. After the news Aimery had given them, Cole could think of nothing else but discovering if Shannon was indeed one of the women needed to end the evil.

He hurried to the tavern and found her scurrying from one table to the next.

Strands of her thick brunette hair fell around her face in disarray. He longed to reach up and smooth them away before kissing her plump lips.

The calm he had drawn from his training was fast dwindling. And when she raised her eyes and spotted him, the smile she gave him made him want to carry her up the stairs and make love to her until morning.

"Hello," she said.

"Hello." He had to tell himself to find a table before he did something foolish like bend her over his arm and kiss her breathless, staking his claim on her for all to see.

He sank into a chair at his favorite table. "You look tired."

"I'm fine," she said.

"Benton paid me a visit. He told me to leave."

Her glance fell away from his. "Will you?" she asked softly.

"Never," he vowed. "I gave you my word, Shannon."

When she again looked at him, her honey brown eyes pooled with relief. "I've found out some more information for you."

"Good. We'll meet at midnight again."

She shook her head. "It needs to be sooner."

"All right. If you cannot find me, tell Gabriel."

"And where are you going to be?"

He shrugged, not wanting to worry her. "Just know that you will be taken care of."

Cole waited until she had walked away before he blew out a breath. When he parted company with Gabriel and Aimery, Gabriel had decided it was time for him to do some snooping on his own. Cole agreed. He had learned nothing in the few days he had walked among the village as a stranger. Mayhap Gabriel's disguise was just what was needed.

Cole's gaze found Shannon. She was a strong, beautiful woman, but everyone had their limits. He had no idea just how much more Shannon could handle, and if what he suspected was true, she was going to have the discovery of a lifetime.

His jaw clenched as he imagined what she had felt at discovering she was no longer in her time, and now a slave to a vicious ruler of a small village in England.

But she had survived it. She had survived weeks amid Benton's nasty temper and meaty fists, with fear always lurking near her, wondering just why she was there.

And Cole couldn't wait to take her away from it all.

However, if she was indeed one of the women they searched for, then she would be taken somewhere where the evil couldn't reach her--and neither would Cole.

He shoved aside that thought and concentrated on formulating a plan to find out if Shannon bore the mark or not.

Shannon covertly watched Cole as she walked about the dining room. He seemed deep in thought, as though he had some great mystery to figure out. She just assumed the great mystery was what kind of creature lurked inside the castle.

The day flew by as if on the wings of a bird, and as night enveloped the small village, Shannon's heart thumped with fear and anticipation. She had much to tell Cole, and she knew some of it would aid him and Gabriel in their quest.

She took her time cleaning the dining room, making sure she kept her eye on the windows to see if she spotted anyone.

"Finish in the morn, wench," Benton boomed from behind her. "You've taken too long."

Shannon gasped as Benton grabbed her arm and dragged her to her room. As she passed the stairs, she saw Cole watching them and silently prayed he wouldn't do anything until Benton left.

Benton pushed her into her room and slammed the door closed. For a moment she feared he might try and lock the door, but instead, she heard his heavy footsteps walk away and then continue out the door.

Just as she was about to rise, she heard someone approach her door. Her first thought was that the castle guards had come to get her, and she nearly started screaming.

Her gaze quickly scanned her small room and found the only weapon available to her--the water bowl. She dumped the water onto the floor and held the bowl over her head as she waited by the door.

The door slowly creaked open, and her heart thundered in her chest. Her arms shook, and her knees began to tremble. But she didn't lose her grip on the water bowl.

As the door opened wider and she saw the shadow of a man move to step into her room, she knew it was now or never. Just as she was about to slam the water bowl against her intruder's head, she spotted the unusual fabric the intruder wore.

It took all her might to stop the downward arc of her hands. She managed it, but also managed to throw herself off balance. Large, strong hands wrapped around her waist and steadied her as she quickly lowered the bowl.

"Expecting someone else?" Cole whispered in her ear.

Excitement replaced her fear as Shannon turned toward Cole's muscular chest and dropped the water bowl. Her hands ran over his sculpted chest, and she sighed with pleasure.

"The material," she said. "It's unlike anything I've ever felt. It's smoother than silk, looks sturdier than the thickest wool, yet it moves beneath my hand as if it's alive."

"Because I'm alive."

She raised her gaze to him. "This," she said as she again ran her hand over the fabric, "wasn't made here."

He shook his head in answer.

Shannon swallowed and licked her lips, unsure if she wanted to know just where the material was from. In the end, her curiosity got the better of her. "Where is it from?"

It seemed Cole was as unsure of answering her as she had been of asking. "Another realm."

"Which one?"

His eyes searched Shannon's and his hands came up and cupped her head on either side. "Are you sure you want to know?"

"Yes."

CHAPTER FIFTEEN

"The Realm of the Fae."

Somehow, Shannon wasn't surprised at Cole's answer. "Then, they really do exist."

He nodded. "Very much so. They raised me and trained me."

"And they also lead the Shields."

The smile that spread across his gorgeous face quickened her heartbeat. "Aye. They do. They are linked to this realm because they once dwelled here. If anything should happen to Earth…"

"Then they would be destroyed as well," she finished.

"Aye."

"Why don't they help more?"

"They can't. There are boundaries in which they must abide. They put the Shields together, arm us, inform us, and at times move us through time, but even that is pressing the limits of what they are allowed to do."

"It doesn't seem fair. If what I heard of the Fae is true, then the battle would be over quickly if they could fight."

"Exactly," Cole said as his thumbs lightly rubbed her jaw. "It's the very reason why this evil doesn't attack the Fae on their realm."

Before she could ask him more, his lips came down on hers, hot and demanding. It was just what Shannon needed. Her arms wrapped around his neck as she drowned in the sensuality that was Cole.

When they parted, both were breathing heavily and there was no mistaking the desire that darkened Cole's eyes. She grinned, loving how much he wanted her.

She knew they were about to make love again. Her heart soared and her body throbbed at the prospect of having Cole's body on hers again.

He pulled her towards him, his eyes scorching in their intensity. His mouth was millimeters away, all she had to do was rise up on her tiptoes and she'd feel his sensuous lips on hers again.

Just as his lips touched hers, they heard it.

The castle guards had arrived.

"I've got to stop them," Cole said as he raced to the window.

She touched his shoulder just as he threw a leg out the window. "Please stay safe."

He gave her a quick kiss. "Always. Now, stay inside, don't look out the window."

Cole prayed she would listen to him, but he feared her curiosity would get the better of her as it always did.

He had his smaller axes in each hand as he ran

from behind the tavern. Just as he expected, Gabriel was already in the fray and taking on two guards at once.

This time twenty men had come to the village. While Gabriel fought, the others surrounded a hut and kicked in the door. Cole's blood boiled when they dragged out a small boy no older than ten summers. When the father tried to stop the guards, he was rewarded by being knocked unconscious and hauled after the boy.

By the time Cole reached them, Gabriel had killed the two guards he fought and turned to more. One spotted Cole and raised his sword. Cole dove and rolled just as the sword sliced through the air. He came to his feet, pivoted, and buried his axe in the guard's back.

The man gave a small cry before he fell lifeless to the ground. Cole quickly kicked the guard off his axe and turned just as a sword came at his neck. Cole lunged back and felt the air as the blade sliced by him.

Cole twirled the axes beside him as he and the guard circled each other. Cole advanced on the guard, and while one axe went toward the guard's side, the other went to his chest.

When the guard fell to the ground as blood pooled out of his wounds, Cole turned and saw Gabriel kill another. The rest of the guards started toward the castle with the father and son.

"There isn't a lot of time," Cole said as they raced after the guards.

"You follow them," Gabriel said as he sheathed his sword and reached for his bow. "I'll meet up with you at the castle."

He gave a nod, and Gabriel disappeared into the forest. Though Gabriel was dangerous with a sword, he was inhuman with his bow. An asset the Shields had used on many occasions.

Cole kept to the shadows, and though the three guards in the back of the group kept looking over their shoulders, they never saw him coming.

He aimed one of the small axes and let it fly. It struck the guard on the right. As the guard fell dead, the others gave a warning shout.

Cole ran to the fallen guard, knelt, and retrieved his bloodied axe. The men had formed one tight huddle, but that didn't deter Cole. He always did like a challenge.

He flexed his hands on the handles of his axes, took his aim, and let both loose. They landed with deadly accuracy in two guards.

Cole reached for his double-headed axe and rose to his feet to chase after the others who raced toward the castle. When the castle gate came into view, Cole knew he had to do everything in his power to stop them from sending the boy and his father to their deaths.

Seven guards halted their retreat and turned to face him while the four holding the father and son continued toward the gate. Cole skidded to a stop half way to the guards and waited. It didn't take them long to attack.

He turned around, gaining momentum in his swing, and sliced the throat of one before embedding his axe in the chest of another. Cole yanked his axe out just in time to duck as a sword swung at his head.

One man aimed a crossbow at him, but before Cole could move out of the way or strike him, the guard fell to his side, an arrow protruding from his back.

Cole smiled, ever thankful for Gabriel's aim, and turned to the other five guards. They circled around him, waiting to attack. Suddenly, two of them dropped to the ground, their open eyes staring unseeing at the sky.

With a wide swing, Cole sliced open the chests of two guards as the last ran toward the castle gates. He didn't get far before Gabriel's arrow landed in his heart.

The last four guards half dragged, half carried the father and son to the gate as they realized they were the only guards remaining.

Cole ran after them, grabbing his two smaller axes on the way. The guards were nearly to the gate. He quickly sheathed the two small axes as he lengthened his strides. As he neared, he spotted Gabriel off to the side of the castle.

If Cole failed, Gabriel would not.

He saw Gabriel ready his bow, and Cole quickly knelt, unsheathed his dagger, and let it fly the same time Gabriel released his bowstring. Cole's blade landed in the guard that held the boy, while Gabriel's arrow hit the guard holding the father.

Cole stood, smiling. With the boy struggling, the one guard couldn't hold him, and with the father unconscious, his guard couldn't drag his weight.

They would have to choose. Father or son.

The man holding the boy cuffed him viciously

across the face, sending the boy tumbling to the ground. Cole clenched his jaw and palmed an axe in each hand. He knew Gabriel would reach the boy, so Cole sprinted the last distance between him and the guards.

They weren't expecting him.

He sliced one on the back of the knee with his axe, and when the other turned toward him, he elbowed him in the face. Both guards fell to the ground.

Cole spotted more men leaning over the gatehouse, readying their bows. He needed to get the boy and father and hide quickly.

"Come on," he whispered urgently to the boy as he hefted the father on his shoulders and raced to the trees.

The boy scrambled to his feet and hurried to follow.

Cole almost made it to the trees when he felt a searing pain. His shoulder spasmed with a burning pain that quickly spread through his body. His arms weakened, and it was all he could do to hold on to the boy's father.

He focused on the trees and the boy beside him as he kept running. Gabriel was waiting for him, but Cole wouldn't stop.

"We have to find a safe place. They'll be looking for us," he said as he hurried past Gabriel who scooped up the boy in his arms.

He had no idea how long they walked or when Gabriel had moved ahead of him. All Cole knew was that the flesh around his shoulder felt as if it were on fire. The longer he stayed on his feet, the more difficult it became to keep moving. Several times he stumbled, but managed to stay on his feet. His luck gave out when his toe caught on a root and his legs gave out.

Cole fell to his knees, and his hold on the father gave out. In an instant, Gabriel was beside him. Cole couldn't lift his head to look at his friend. The fire raging in his body drowned out anything else.

"We're stopping. Here. Now."

"Nay," Cole said. He shook his head, wondering why Gabriel's voice sounded like it came from deep within a tunnel.

"Don't be foolish," Gabriel snapped. "If they're tracking us, they'll find us with as slow as we've gone." He set the boy on the ground next to his father.

Cole slowly got to his feet with the help of a tree, but was unable to move his left shoulder at all now. He tried to squeeze his hand, but even that didn't obey him.

"Where are you hurt?" Gabriel asked.

"Tend to the father and son first."

Gabriel stood in front of Cole, his face a mask of anger in the moonlight. "Where are you injured?" he asked again.

"My shoulder," Cole finally answered.

He waited as Gabriel moved to his back. "How bad is it?" he asked. Silence.

"Gabriel."

"We need to move somewhere safer."

Cole didn't like Gabriel's tone or the fact he wouldn't answer his question. He turned to his friend. "Gabriel."

He waited until Gabriel turned to look at him

before he continued. "Take out the arrow."

"Nay."

"Why not."

Gabriel glanced at the ground and took a deep breath. "There is poison on the arrow. I don't know what kind yet, and I cannot take the chance of treating you now. We need to get somewhere safe."

The problem was, there was nowhere safe.

Cole struggled to keep his eyes open. "We cannot return to the tavern. They'll know it was us."

"Not unless we get there before them," Gabriel said as he bent and picked up the boy. "Aimery."

As quick as lightening Aimery stood before them. "You have news?"

"Nay," Gabriel answered. "There isn't much time. Cole is injured, and I can't carry the father as well as the son."

Cole leaned against the tree as Aimery's gaze swung to him. With each breath that passed through Cole's body, it became harder and harder to stay on his feet and focused on his duty.

"I'll get the boy and his father to safety," Aimery said as he took the boy from Gabriel. "Get Cole to the tavern. Quickly."

"You cannot return the boy and the father to the village," Cole said.

Neither answered him as Gabriel slung an arm around him and steered him toward the village.

"Move, Cole," Gabriel ground out.

Cole did his best to stay upright. He forgot how many times he tripped, the agony of his shoulder squeezing every last drop of his strength.

Suddenly, through the trees, he spotted the tavern. As his eyes closed, his last thought was of Shannon.

CHAPTER SIXTEEN

Shannon couldn't sit still as she worried if Cole and Gabriel had managed to save whoever it was that had been taken. If she were a nail biter, her fingers would be gnawed to her first knuckle.

As it was, all she could do was pace and worry--something she was awfully good at.

She jumped off the bed when she heard the scratch at her window. There were only two men who would dare to come to her window. She raced over to discover if it was Cole or Gabriel, praying all the while that it was Cole.

Her heart fell to her feet like a stone when she saw Gabriel holding an unconscious Cole over his shoulders.

"What happened?" she asked.

"I'll explain later. Help me get him inside," Gabriel said as he struggled to shift Cole.

Shannon took Cole's feet and lifted them through the window as Gabriel held his upper body. Once Cole was mostly through the window, Shannon situated herself where she was able to hold Cole up while Gabriel climbed through. Her heart hammered in her chest as she feared Benton would crash through her door at any moment.

She had never realized how heavy Cole was, but she quickly forgot that as she spotted the arrow protruding from his back. Her throat burned with unshed tears as Gabriel took Cole out of her arms and laid him on his stomach on the bed.

"I'll move him to his chamber as soon as I get the arrow out and decipher what poison was used."

The room tilted around Shannon. "Poison?"

"Get me water," Gabriel said in response. "Now."

Once Shannon returned with the water, Gabriel bade her get strips of cloth and hot water. She then stood and watched as Gabriel cut Cole's vest and tunic away to reveal the wound.

Already, the flesh around his wound oozed puss and had turned a nasty green.

"I've seen this before," Gabriel mumbled.

It was the only good bit of news. "Can you help him?"

Gabriel nodded as he pulled out his black bag from his vest and unrolled it.

Shannon's gaze was riveted on Cole and how deathly still he lay upon her bed. "I thought Cole was immortal."

Gabriel gave her a sharp look. "He is, but everyone can be killed by dark magic."

"What a comfort," she whispered to herself as Gabriel set out his herbs and then turned Cole onto his side.

When Gabriel reached for the arrow, Shannon held her breath. Her fingernails dug into her palms as he grasped the arrow and pushed it through until the arrowhead jutted from Cole's chest.

"Hold him," Gabriel urged.

Shannon sat on the bed and held Cole against her, noting his usually tan skin had a paleness to it that frightened her. She had seen numerous wounds as an EMT in Chicago, and could tell that this one was bad. Very bad.

Her stomach rolled as Gabriel broke off the head of the arrow and threw it to the floor. He then reached around and grasped the shaft, and with one good pull, yanked it free from Cole's body.

She shifted her gaze from Cole's wound to Gabriel as he mixed herbs and other unknown things together. He made one into a paste which he spread on Cole's wounds and then wrapped a bandage around them.

"Lay him down," Gabriel said as he turned back to his herbs.

Slowly, Shannon moved and let Cole lay on his back. She was about to ask Gabriel what he had planned when he turned to them with a mug full of some liquid.

"He needs to drink this. All of it."

"All right," Shannon said and waited. It took her a moment to realize Gabriel wanted her to get it down Cole. She licked her lips and reached for the mug.

Gabriel rose to his feet. "I'll return shortly, after I make sure no one is in his chamber. Get that down him by the time I return."

Shannon didn't have time to blink before Gabriel was gone. She reached over and smoothed the hair from Cole's forehead.

"I don't like seeing you like this. You told me you were immortal, and where I come from, that means nothing short of hacking off your head will kill you."

She adjusted herself so that she sat closer to his face. After moving her hand under his neck, she tilted up his head, parted his lips, and put the mug to his mouth.

When she tried to get the liquid down him, it spilled out the corners of his mouth.

"No, Cole. Drink for me," she said as she laid her forehead against his. "Please. Drink for me."

She straightened and tried again, this time getting some into his mouth, but spilling more out.

By now, tears fell from her eyes. She was going to fail, and because of her, Cole would die. Silently, she screamed at herself. She was an EMT, a person trained to save lives, but she wasn't trained on magic or immortals.

She took a deep breath and dashed the tears from her face. Then she moved near Cole's ear. "Listen to me, Cole. I'm going to put this mug against your lips, pour the liquid into your mouth, and you're going to swallow. I refuse to let you die on me. Please. I'm begging you. I need you."

This time, she sent a silent prayer to God to help her get the liquid down. She gave Cole a light kiss and then placed the mug to his lips. With one last brief prayer, she tilted the cup.

To her relief, he swallowed.

Elation ran through her. Each time she put the liquid in his mouth, he swallowed. She didn't know what had worked and didn't care. By the time Gabriel returned, she just finished putting the last of the medicine in Cole's mouth.

"He drank it?" Gabriel asked, incredulous.

Shannon slowly nodded, drained emotionally and mentally. "You sound surprised."

"None of us have ever gotten him to drink it."

Shannon chuckled and ran her hand down the side of Cole's face. "I refused to give up." When she looked at Gabriel, his intense stare unsettled her. "Did I do something wrong?"

"Actually," he said softly. "You've done everything right. Let's move him to his chamber."

She went to the door as Gabriel once more put Cole over his shoulders as a fireman carried victims. When they finally got Cole into his room and on his bed, she let out a sigh of relief.

"Hurry and return to your chamber," Gabriel warned.

Shannon didn't want to leave Cole, but she knew she must. Reluctantly, she backed out of the room and returned to hers.

Cole opened his eyes and found everything around him unfocused and hazy. He blinked several times and tried again. Slowly, his eyes came into focus while he looked around his chamber. By the light, he could tell that the sun was just beginning to rise. Instantly, images of the previous night flashed into his mind, including his wound.

He tested his shoulder gingerly and found it sore but nothing like it had been.

"How do you feel?"

Cole allowed his gaze to move to the window where Gabriel lounged. "Like I was stampeded by dragons."

Gabriel chuckled. "The poison used was the same poison given to Mina."

Cole vividly remembered how Mina, Hugh's wife, had nearly died from the vicious black magic. "I owe you my thanks again."

"No need," Gabriel said and moved to the table where he reached for a mug. "Time to drink."

"You know I don't drink that."

Gabriel raised a black brow and stared at him. "You did last night. For Shannon."

That brought Cole up short. "What?"

"I gave it to her to give her something to do while I dispatched the guards around the tavern and inspected your chamber. By the time I returned, she had the entire thing down you."

"What is in that liquid anyway?"

Gabriel grinned. "Let's just say that it's a bit stronger than the mug of medicine I gave you for your knife wound."

Cole sat up and swung his legs over the bed. "Let's hope it did its job, since I know I'll be receiving a visit from Gyles today."

"No doubt."

"Did you happen to see who shot the arrow?"

Gabriel shook his head. "Wish I had. These men aren't playing around. I think it's time we did something about it instead of waiting for them."

"I agree. How did your disguise work yesterday?"

Gabriel laughed. "No one suspected a thing. I discovered the town is terrified of the baron. Everyone knows there is something in the castle, but no one knows what. What Shannon told you is correct. No one is allowed to leave the village."

"Interesting."

"Aye. By the way, I heard there was a man that might be able to give us even more information. I think I'll pay him a visit today."

"Get back here as soon as you can. After last night, I have a feeling the guards won't wait until midnight."

A roar split the air then, loud and long, as if all the fury of the realm was being released in that bellow. Gabriel and Cole exchanged a look before Gabriel slipped out the window and down the wall.

Cole rose from the bed and saw his tattered tunic and leather jerkin on the floor. Thankfully, being a Shield, the Fae took care of clothes in case something like this happened, which was quite often.

Sure enough, when Cole looked at the end of the bed, another tunic and jerkin awaited him. He stretched his arm as far as he could, needing to know his limitations before they were put to the test.

He normally rebounded from a wound faster than this, but black magic had been used. Which meant there was no telling exactly what it had done to him, or when he would fully recover.

His gaze caught sight of the mug awaiting him on

the table. Maybe Gabriel's brew had helped, and if the guards attacked tonight, Cole was going to need to be healthy.

Gabriel never failed them when it came to healing, but being immortal, Cole left the mixtures to the mortals. Now, though, his mind was changed. He picked up the mug and drained the contents.

It left a slightly bitter taste in his mouth, but was worth it if he was indeed fully healed by nightfall.

He unwrapped the bandage and saw the wound healing as it always did. Once his inspection of the wounds was done, he donned his tunic and jerkin, noting his ruined clothes had vanished, and made for the door. And Shannon.

Shannon had information for him that she hadn't been able to share last night.

CHAPTER SEVENTEEN

Shannon hurried from one table to the next, Benton barking in her ears the entire time. She was exhausted from the night before, and desperately worried about Cole. Try as she might, she hadn't been able to check on him that morning. Every time she tried to go up the stairs, Benton was there.

She even attempted to catch Gabriel as he walked past the tavern, which had earned her a good yelling from Benton that still had her ears ringing.

As she moved away from a table, she backed into someone. Silently cursing her luck, she turned, intending to apologize, when she heard the deep voice that always managed to make her a puddle of goo.

"I beg your pardon," Cole said, his voice low.

Shannon jerked, amazed to see him standing after the wound he had received. She knew people stared, but she couldn't stop the smile from showing.

"It was my fault actually. May I get you something to eat?" she asked, wishing they were alone so she could fling herself at him and kiss every inch of him.

"Aye. I'm famished."

She hurried to get his food, eager for just a moment alone with him so she could see how he really felt. Her hand reached for the plate when Benton's meaty fisted closed around her wrist.

Her gaze jerked to his. "What have I done this time?" she asked, not trying to hide the irritation in her voice. She wanted to speak with Cole, and Benton dared to detain her.

"I want you to find out what he's doing here. The baron wants the information immediately."

Shannon swallowed. "You want me to spy for you?"

He nodded slowly. "Do you have a problem with that? Should I take you in the back and change your mind?"

"No," she quickly replied. "I'm just curious why you are interested in him."

Benton's gaze moved over her shoulder, then back at her. "The reason is none of your business, wench. Get the information, and you'll be rewarded."

"With my freedom?"

"Nay. You'll be allowed to live another day," he said and released her.

Shannon took the plate of food and walked to Cole. "Don't look at Benton," she said as she sat the plate down.

"What did he want with you?"

She met his chocolate brown gaze. "He wants me to spy for him."

The smile that spread over Cole's face made her

knees weak.

"Just what I was hoping for."

"What? Are you nuts?"

"I have no nuts," he said softly.

Shannon shook her head in irritation at his jest. "Are you crazy? Mad?"

He laughed, the sound pouring over her like a warm blanket on a cool autumn day. His hand reached out and took hers. "This allows us to spend more time together. No more hiding."

It dawned on her then. "You wanted this."

"I'd hoped the baron would ask for information, and who better to get it out of me than the woman I stopped from a beating the first night I arrived."

"Amazing."

"I try," he said with a wink.

She laughed, unable to stop herself. "So, what's the next plan?"

He continued to smile, but the light had faded from his gaze. "I need the information you were going to give me last eve."

She'd completely forgotten about that. "I can't do it here. We need to be alone."

"That can be arranged," he said as he released her hand and reached for his fork. "Tell Benton I've requested you in my chamber in an hour."

As she walked from his table, she couldn't believe Benton wouldn't know she was really helping Cole and Gabriel. Could the man be that dense?

"Well," Benton said as she entered the kitchen.

She shrugged. "It seems our visitor has taken a fancy to me."

Benton snorted loudly. "That was obvious the first night he arrived. Did you learn anything?"

"Not yet. He has asked me to his chamber in an hour."

"Make sure you're there," Benton said as he turned on his heel.

Shannon blinked. Acting had never been her forte. In truth, she nearly failed drama class in high school, but somehow she had managed to pull off this little stunt. For now. The longer it continued, the more lies they spun, the trickier it would become.

If they wanted to escape with their lives, Shannon was going to have to be extra careful.

Their very lives depended upon it.

"Nothing like a little stress to keep me on my toes," she mumbled as she picked up more plates to deliver.

Cole counted the moments until it was time for Shannon's arrival. He sat, he twiddled his thumbs, he paced, he sharpened his axes, and he even tried to sleep. Yet, it was all impossible.

When the soft knock sounded on his door, he leapt from the bed and yanked it open to see Shannon standing before him, a bright smile on her face.

"Hello," she said.

"Hello."

Her smile widened. "May I come in?"

He stepped back to allow her entry before barring the door. "Does he suspect?" he whispered.

She shook her head. "Not at all."

"Good," Cole replied as he dragged her against him.

He slanted his mouth over hers and plunged his tongue inside her mouth. When she sighed and wrapped her arms around his neck, it was all he could do not to take her right then.

Her kisses left him weak and strong at the same time. No woman had ever affected him this way. Usually, by this time, he had had his fill and was looking for someone new. Yet, his gaze hadn't strayed from Shannon.

And he feared it never would.

He broke the kiss, his body shaking with need, and stepped away from her.

"What did you discover?" he asked.

She closed her eyes and sank onto the bed. "Gyles is power hungry. He journeyed to a sacred place, a place said to be haunted now, and when he returned, he dominated the entire village."

"Where is this place?"

She shrugged her dainty shoulders. "I don't know. They talked as though it wasn't that far away."

"Did they describe anything?" If he could just get some information about the area, Aimery would be able to help them find it.

She shook her head. "Just kept saying it was a sacred place, a place no one went to anymore. I gathered that most feared it."

Cole thought a moment. "Mayhap Gabriel will be able to tell us more when he returns. As for the power Gyles has over the village, it is derived from a blue stone."

"What kind of stone?"

"It is smooth as silk, the blue indescribable in its beauty, and no larger than the palm of a child's hand. It's with that stone that he controls the creature."

"Oh," she said and bit her lip as she thought over his words. "What if we destroy the stone?"

"Destroying the stone is one of our goals. It must be destroyed or someone else will call up another creature."

"Will destroying the stone kill the creature that is here?"

Cole nodded. "Aye. However, from what we've learned of our missions, the stone is usually hidden."

"What if I went in to find it?"

Her bravery astounded him. He knelt in front of her, cupping her face in his hands. "You are doing entirely too much now. I hate that we put you in this position."

"It was my choice," she reminded him.

"Aye, but we would've kept you until you changed your mind. Our time here is drawing to an end. I can feel it in the air. After we thwarted the guards last night, there is going to be Hell to pay today."

"I know," she said with a sigh. "Every villager who has come to the tavern is frightened. I can see it in their eyes."

"They should be frightened. I've a feeling the creature will be let loose this night. The entire village will be slaughtered."

"Oh, my God."

"It's the goal of the creature. It's why it was summoned. The only reason I can conclude why Gyles hasn't let the creature loose yet, is because he likes the power the stone gives him."

"Can you stop the creature?"

"Aye."

"Aren't you frightened?" she asked, her eyes wide with fear.

Cole shook his head and rose to his feet. "This is what the Shields do. We took an oath to protect this realm, and we'll do that to our dying breath."

Her brows drew together as she thought over his words. "I understand. You gave your oath to the Fae, but that doesn't mean you can't be frightened."

"I've never been afraid for my own life, Shannon. I've never known fear until you. Now I worry for your life, and if I'll be able to keep you alive."

He walked to the window, his back to her. "I was but a small child when they found me wandering between realms. Mine had been destroyed by the very evil attempting to destroy yours. The Fae took me in as their own."

The feel of her hands on his back was like a bolt of lightning rushing through him.

"Can you recall nothing of your realm?"

"Nay." Not for lack of trying on his part. He wanted something, anything he could remember of his world, his family. But his mind blocked out everything of that time. His memories started with the day Aimery found him.

"I'm so sorry," she said and laid her head on his back. "I also know nothing of my family. I was adopted by a decent family, but soon after adopting me they had kids of their own."

Her words startled him. He turned towards her. "Did they treat you ill?"

She smiled sadly. "Not at all. Maybe it was just me, but I never truly felt a part of them. Once they adopted me, they couldn't very well give me back. They thought they would never have kids of their own."

"Do you still have contact with them?"

"No. Carol died when I was seventeen, and Mack turned his attention to his children. After I graduated from high school, I moved to Chicago where I went to college at night and worked during the day as an Emergency Medical Technician. I had just gotten my degree in marketing a couple of months ago, and was about to start looking for a new job when I ended up here."

He tilted her face to his and searched her eyes. The sadness he saw there disturbed him, making him want to erase it all. "We will return you to your time."

She shrugged. "Does it really matter? I have no family, no job. I have nothing to return to."

"No man has claimed you?"

She laughed. "Between my job and college, I rarely had time to do laundry, much less date."

"Date?"

"Go out with men. So no, no man has laid claim to me."

"Good," Cole said and he kissed her. When they pulled apart, both were panting and eager for more. "Not yet," he said as he captured her hands. "There is more we need to discuss."

"Like what?" she asked as she rose up on her

tiptoes and kissed his neck.

Her warm tongue and hot breath scalded him to his toes. "Shannon," he moaned, not sure how long he could hold her off.

"Please, Cole. My body burns for yours."

Her words were his undoing. He crushed her to him, molding her lush body to his. Her moans only drove him onward, seeking to fill her with one thought—him.

CHAPTER EIGHTEEN

Shannon's body was on fire. Each kiss, each caress, each hungry look she saw in Cole's eyes only ignited her further. Her body seemed attuned to his, and with the slightest look, she was wet and panting for him.

And she loved it.

For many years, she thought herself incapable of experiencing sex like a normal woman, but then she found Cole. Cole, a woman's greatest sensual desire, was kissing her as if there were no tomorrow, as if she were the only woman in the universe for him.

A sigh escaped her as his magical hands roamed her body, finding hidden places that sent her reeling with desire. The man was a walking sex god.

His hands cupped her breasts and massaged them as he rubbed his rod against her. She felt moisture flood her panties, and yearned to feel his flesh against hers.

"I have to have you now," Cole said in her ear just before he lifted her off her feet.

Shannon immediately wrapped her legs around his waist, eager to help him move her heavy skirts out of the way. Her eyes caught his gaze and wondered at the look in them. There was desire, yes, but something else, something she couldn't quite name.

They gazed at each other in silence. Somehow, Shannon knew this moment was special and was most likely a moment she would never know again.

When she could take no more, she leaned forward and kissed him, sliding her tongue past his full, wide lips and into his mouth. His tongue readily mated with hers, his intoxicating taste making her wild with yearning and wanton with desire.

He turned her from a frigid, frightened woman into a lust-craved maniac who was eager to please.

When his hands moved to the front of her gown and lowered it so her breasts popped free, she anxiously waited to feel his calloused hands on them, stroking, kneading, squeezing. Her nipples hardened as his hands grazed her flesh.

His expert touch, both sensual and gentle, knew exactly what would drive her wild. He kneaded one breast while he squeezed her nipple on the other. The exquisite torture left her dazed and wanting more. She never felt him pull down her bra, only felt his hot tongue as he swirled a nipple in his mouth and gently suckled.

By now she was breathless, nearly crying out from the throbbing between her legs, an ache that intensified with each lick of Cole's tongue on her nipples. Her need for release drove her onward, when she would have otherwise been mortified to find herself up against a wall with a man about to make love to her.

Her hands shoved aside his leather vest and ran over his tunic, the feel of the fabric warming her hands, sending little pulses through her.

Cole ground his rod against her aching sex, and she cried out.

"Now," she sobbed. "Please, Cole. Take me now."

With the slightest movement, he shifted her, unlaced his trousers, and sprang free. Her hands moved to touch him, but he stopped her.

"If you touch me now, I will spill my seed. I need you too desperately."

She knew exactly how he felt, but she was determined to know the feel of him soon. She devised her plan as he moved aside her panties.

Those thoughts soon scattered as the tip of Cole's rod entered her. She wanted him to fill her fully, but he wouldn't allow her to move her hips, keeping her steady with his big hands as he slowly moved in and out of her with short strokes, never giving her more than an inch or two of him.

The more he moved, the more friction he caused between them, and the higher she rose. His mouth moved over her neck and breasts, continually giving her pleasure.

Just when she didn't think she could take much more, he thrust deep, filling her completely. Shannon sighed, her forehead against his as her sex expanded and clutched around him.

"I love the feel of you inside me," she whispered.

"Not as much as I love being inside of you."

She looked into his eyes, loving the desire she saw

there. And when he began to rotate his hips, she dug her nails into his shoulders as she felt herself building toward her climax.

Each time she got close, he would alter his movements, bringing her greater pleasure. Sweat glistened off them when he finally began to thrust into her harder, deeper than before.

All too soon, her climax hit. She leaned her head back against the wall and closed her eyes as her body convulsed around him. When he too climaxed, she held him tight and felt his seed pour into her.

"You're amazing," she whispered in his ear.

He smiled as he moved them away from the wall to the bed. He pulled out of her just before he laid her on the bed. Shannon curled into his side. She was happy, something she thought never to be again. She wondered what the future held for her, and if Cole would be in it.

"Do you have a mark on you?"

Cole's words jarred her out of her thoughts. She lifted her head from his shoulder and looked at him. "What?"

"A mark. Sort of like a birthmark. Do you have one?"

She shook her head. "Not that I know of. Why?"

"We are searching for a woman with just such a mark."

"Why?" The need to know was overwhelming.

Cole glanced away. "She's part of all of this. Many years ago, there was a realm about to be destroyed by the evil. They had knowledge that could kill the evil, but didn't have time to carry out the plan. They chose twelve infants, six boys and six girls, to give that knowledge to. Those babies were sent to this realm in different times and places."

"You need to find them to end this."

He nodded. "We've found two already."

"Two out of twelve isn't so great," she said.

"All of the boys died in either wars, plagues, or duels."

Shannon rolled her eyes. "Somehow I'm not surprised. And the girls? Do all six still live?"

He shrugged. "We know two still live, and another died from the plague, but we know nothing of the other three. Two of the other Shields, the ones that traveled to your time, found another of the women."

"Really?" Her mind ran wild with what he told her. There were actually women walking around from another realm. It was too weird and too neat.

"Aye. So, why did you think I might be one of them?" Secretly, she wished she were. It would explain how she was never able to find her birth mother.

"The evil knows of the women now, and to thwart us, he's sending the creatures to where they are, bringing them back through time to kill them."

Shannon's stomach flopped like a fish out of water. "And you think that's why I was brought here? Why couldn't he kill the women in the future?"

"He's too weak there. Here, in this time, he is his strongest."

"Lucky guy," she grumbled. She turned her gaze to Cole. "I wish I was the woman you seek. It would help you fight the evil."

He nodded. "I'd assumed you were, but if you

aren't, then Gyles brought you back for another reason."

She laid her head on his shoulder again and replayed his words over and over. "How many of the women do you need to kill the evil?"

"No less than four, but the more we have, the greater their power will be."

"What do they have to do?"

He sighed loudly. "We don't know yet."

"I always hated flying blind. Not knowing what you're facing or exactly how to kill it can lead to mistakes."

She felt him nod. "And mistakes we cannot afford to make."

"Then we better act fast."

Before Cole could respond, a small rock came flying through the window.

"Fix yourself," he ordered as he rushed from the bed.

Shannon quickly adjusted her skirts and put her breasts back into her bra, and then into the bodice of her gown. She pushed her hair away from her face and faced the window just as a man climbed in.

He was at least in his early fifties, with thick salt and pepper hair and a beard that covered his entire face. His clothes were that of the villagers, yet his were more frayed and used, as though they were the only ones he had. No weapons could be seen on his body, and by the looks of him, she wondered how he managed to climb up the tavern into the room.

She looked from the stranger to Cole, waiting for Cole to introduce them. She had assumed the only other man with him was Gabriel, but maybe she had been wrong.

"Did you find out anything?" Cole asked.

The stranger nodded his head as he went to the chair and sank into it.

Shannon walked to the stranger and held out her hand. "I'm Shannon O'Malley."

The stranger raised silver eyes to her, eyes that were somehow familiar, and smiled broadly. "Guess my disguise works."

Shannon looked over her shoulder at Cole and waited for him to tell her what was going on. The stranger took her hand, and she jerked back around to him.

"Nice to meet you again, Shannon."

As soon as the words fell from his lips, her mouth gaped open. "Gabriel?"

He laughed and pulled the beard from his face. Next came the hair and a fake nose. She was too stunned to think about him having that kind of costuming to ask him where he had gotten it. Instead, she marveled at his transformation.

Cole moved to stand beside Shannon. Her reaction to Gabriel had been amusing.

It was sometimes hard to tell who he was when he went under disguise, but Cole had learned to look for Gabriel's striking silver eyes.

"What have you learned?" Cole asked.

The smile vanished from Gabriel's face. He rose and went to the water bowl where he washed his face and wet his hair. "The village will be attacked tonight. Several families are going to try and make a run for it since word is spreading like wildfire that the creature will be let loose."

"No more word on what the Viking is doing here?"

Gabriel sighed and turned to Cole. "I'm not so sure that there ever was a Viking."

"You saw the horned helmet and the fur cloak."

"Aye," Gabriel agreed, "but if there was a Viking here, why haven't we seen him? He isn't the creature. He would be aiding the castle guards, not hiding in the castle."

He had a point. Cole knew their options were running out. "I think it's time we put my plan into action."

"Aye."

Cole expected Gabriel to argue, so when he readily agreed, it sent up warning signals. "Why so eager?"

"Someone has to go in."

Cole nodded. "I've already got Gyles' ire. It'll be me."

"Nay," Shannon whispered, the stricken look on her face a blow to his heart.

Cole turned toward her. "I have to go in and find answers."

"Someone has to go in," Gabriel said, "and that someone will be me."

Cole looked to Gabriel. "Nay."

"Aye," Gabriel thundered. "You need to make sure you get Shannon out of here while I'm being taken to the castle. I'll meet you inside."

"It's insane."

"And you taking my place isn't?"

"Stop," Shannon said as she paced the floor.

"Surely there has to be another way."

"There isn't," Cole said as he stood and walked to her. "You have done all you can. It's time to get you back to your own time, and for us to discover just what kind of creature is in the castle walls."

She shook her head. "I can get you more information."

He ran a hand down her cheek. "You've risked your life enough. I promised you freedom, and freedom you shall have."

"Use me as bait," she tried.

Gabriel finished wiping his face and turned to them. "Before, the creatures always attacked us, giving us ample time to study them, but this one, this one is being kept on a very short tether. All that changes tonight. This village will be destroyed. Every life we can save is worth anything that'll happen to us."

Cole, seeing a protest coming, put a finger to Shannon's lips to quiet her. "Go below. Tell Benton you discovered it was me who thwarted the castle guards twice now. Then, I want you to be ready. As soon as I can, I'll get you out of here. Promise me."

He hated the tears that welled up in her eyes, tears he felt.

"I promise," she whispered before she turned and left the chamber.

CHAPTER NINETEEN

Gabriel waited for several hours before he was able to get near Shannon at the tavern. She still didn't recognize him in his new disguise as she placed a tankard of ale in front of him.

"Shannon."

She jerked and lifted her gaze to him. She searched his eyes a moment. "Gabriel?"

"Aye. I need you to help me."

"What?" she asked as she acted as if she was cleaning his table.

"Help me keep Cole away from the castle. I'll make sure Gyles takes me, I just need Cole occupied."

She lifted her gaze to him. "I don't like the idea of either of you going in alone."

"I know, but they'd never take both of us. Cole's mind is full of you, he won't be thinking straight. I have a better chance of getting out of there alive."

He waited for several moments before she finally nodded. "Don't make me regret it."

Gabriel let out the breath he had been holding and

drained the tankard. Cole would never forgive him for this, but it was worth it to keep his friend alive.

Le Blanc Castle was as silent as a tomb, just the way Gyles preferred it. Everyone feared him, respected him. About bloody time, too.

He walked down the dark hallway to the back of the castle. The beast had summoned him. Him! Gyles had nearly ignored the summons. However, something told him to go see what the animal had to say.

The guards at the back door jerked to attention. "Milord," they said in unison.

"Open it," he ordered.

Gyles watched as they unlocked the iron gate. It creaked open, the sound echoing loudly around him. After a deep breath, the great baron of Le Blanc Castle strode into the black as pitch hallway with the stench of death lingering in the air.

"I didn't think you'd come."

The deep baritone of the voice behind him startled Gyles. Though he had complete control over the creature, it still frightened him. Oh, he would never admit that to anyone, but there was no denying the quaking of his heart anytime he neared the beast.

Slowly, Gyles turned around and raised his gaze to the beast. "Why did you think I wouldn't come?"

The laugh, evil to the core, cackled around him. "You can barely tolerate looking at me. Do I scare you that much?"

"You do not frighten me."

A large hairy hand, thrice the size of a normal man's hand, wrapped around Gyles' throat. Part of him wanted to flee immediately, but he knew what the Beast was doing.

"Release me. Now," he demanded.

Instantly, the hand was removed. "You can deny it all you want, my lord, but the quickening of your heartbeat when I am near gives you away."

Gyles grew more uncomfortable. "What is the reason you called for me?"

"I've spoken with Him."

"Him?" Gyles reeled back. "What did he want?"

The Beast crossed his huge arms over his thick chest and glared at Gyles. "'Tis because you are incompetent and don't realize just who is in that village."

Gyles mimicked the Beast and crossed his arms over his chest. "Then tell me."

"Two of the Shields."

Gyles shrugged. "What does that mean for me?"

The Beast let out a roar and flung his arms open, his hot breath coming out in blasts from his nose. "Didn't you listen to anything you were told? The Shields are here to destroy me and your blue stone. They have succeeded in thwarting many of the Master's plans."

"You worry overmuch," Gyles said as he uncrossed his arms and walked to the door. "Which two are these so called Shields?"

"Cole and Gabriel."

Gyles rubbed his chin with his thumb and forefinger. "I know which one Cole is. This other...Gabriel...might be a little trickier to find, but I have a plan to bring them out of hiding as well as giving you a treat."

The Beast laughed. "Let me loose. I will take care of them."

"I'm not ready for you to kill everyone yet."

The Beast snorted. "The Master won't wait much longer. Having control over the stone and me meant you had to annihilate your village."

"I'll take care of the Master when the time comes," Gyles all but spat. He stalked from the hallway through the open door. As the great door was shut and barred behind him he heard the Beast let out another roar.

I am in charge here. I rule this castle and village. Me. No one else.

He started for the stairs that would take him to the great hall. It was time to bring in the Shields.

Cole stood in the trees behind the tavern. He watched Shannon through the open windows. With a sigh, he turned and found Aimery standing beside him.

"You called?" the Fae asked.

Cole nodded. "The creature will destroy the town tonight. Before that happens, I've got a plan to get me into the castle, but I need for Shannon to be returned to her time first."

"Did you find the mark?"

"She doesn't have it," Cole said and ran his hand through his hair. "I haven't yet determined why she was brought here or who the woman is we search for, but I will."

Aimery's Fae blue eyes regarded him solemnly. "How deeply do you feel for Shannon?"

Cole looked away. "More than I would like to."

"I see."

Cole had to have Aimery's word. He faced the Fae commander again. "Will you take her out of here and return her to her own time?"

"Aye. She doesn't belong here and was brought against her will. Just call. I'll be waiting."

With that, Aimery disappeared. Cole raked a hand down his face and looked to the sky. The day had flown by. Noon had already come and gone, and afternoon was creeping upon them. Cole was going to have to be very careful of just how he got Shannon out of the tavern.

He started back toward the tavern when a roar split the air. His fingers flexed on the handle of his war axe. Aye, the time was drawing near. He wanted a look at the creature, and a chance to kill it.

As he walked around the tavern and reached for the door, yet another roar sounded, this one louder, angrier. Cole hesitated a moment before he entered.

His eyes immediately found Gabriel before they swung to Shannon. He gave her a wink, making sure Benton had seen, before he took his usual seat.

Shannon sauntered over to him, a huge smile on her face. "Hungry?" she asked.

"Famished, but not for food."

She laughed, the sound musical to his ears. "I confess, I'm pretty hungry myself."

Cole reached for her hand and ran his thumb over

the back of it. "Did Benton accept what you told him?"

"Oh, yes," she said with a grin. "He wants me to stay near you at all times."

"Just what I hoped for."

"You're impossible."

He smiled, letting his eyes run down her body. "Yet, you like it."

Her smile faltered as she gazed at him. "Yes. I do."

Somehow their playful teasing had shifted, moved into an area Cole couldn't – and wouldn't – venture into. "All the plans in place?"

She nodded woodenly before glancing out the window. "It won't be long now."

"Nay, and then you'll finally be free of this place. I'd take you now, but I don't want Benton to realize you're gone. I need everything to go exactly as I planned it."

She gave him a smile that didn't reach her eyes and took a deep breath. "Let me get you something to drink to pass the time."

He watched as she walked to the bar. When Benton stopped her, Cole wondered if they might get a few moments alone before he brought her to Aimery.

It might be better if he didn't. If he did, he might say something or do something that could only hurt him. Nay, he needed to stay detached as best he could, which was becoming more and more impossible with each moment he spent with her.

How could he, after nearly seven hundred years, have been able to walk away from every woman – until Shannon? What was it about her that drew him like a thirsty man to water?

She was just a woman.

A woman who was incredibly brave and strong and beautiful.

Cole didn't need his conscience to tell him what he already knew. But he was a Shield, a warrior who put his life on the line every day to save the realm of Earth. There wasn't time to have a woman by his side.

He sighed and leaned back in his chair as Shannon approached with his mug of ale. "What did Benton want?"

"To see if you were interested in spending more time with me. He wants more information."

"Then we'll be sure he thinks he's getting it."

Her head tilted to the side. "What do you have in mind?"

"Some more time alone." He tried to stop himself from saying the words, but they were out of his mouth before he could halt them.

Her eyes twinkled with excitement. "I thought you'd never ask."

He couldn't stop the laugh that erupted from him. Despite their grave situation, she teased and jested with him as if everything was fine. She was a remarkable woman, and he was going to hate to see her go. But she had to leave.

"Come," she said and took his hand.

He raised a brow. "Now?"

"Is there a better time?" she asked over her shoulder as she pulled him from his chair and led him to her chamber.

Cole threw Benton a smile as they walked past him.

Not even the mean brute's sneer could dampen Cole's mood. He was given one more moment alone with Shannon, and he was going to make the most of it.

He stepped into her chamber and watched as she closed and barred the door. Her honey brown eyes glittered with passion, and he longed to bury himself inside of her.

All humor fled as he stared into her eyes. He knew he would never see her again after this night, and it disturbed him immensely. He was going to memorize every inch of her body, kiss every inch of her, and love every inch of her.

His heart thumped loudly in his chest, and his body tingled with anticipation. He took a step toward Shannon and reached up to loosen the pins holding her hair. Her thick, dark tresses fell around her shoulders, and he combed his fingers through them.

"I'm going to miss you."

She put her finger to his lips. "Don't talk of that. Not now. Let us pretend the troubles outside that door aren't there, that we are lovers with a bright future ahead of us."

His breath hitched in his throat as she disrobed to stand in front of him with only the lacy under-things she wore on. He reached for her, dismayed to see his hands tremble.

Her warm, silken skin glided beneath his hands as she stepped into his arms. She rose up on her toes and wrapped her arms around his neck as their lips met.

The kiss held desperation, at least it did for Cole. It was the first time he had ever wished he wasn't a Shield. The thought of letting Shannon go nearly doubled him over.

When her hands moved to shove off his jerkin, he let it fall to the floor, and then he helped her remove his tunic, breaking the kiss only long enough to pull it over his head.

He couldn't stand to be apart from her for more than a heartbeat. He backed to the bed until his knees hit. He broke the kiss and slowly sank onto the bed.

"Have I ever told you how beautiful you are?"

She smiled softly. "No."

He ran his hand from her face to her hair. "Of all the things I've seen, you are by far the most stunning in this realm or the Fae realm."

Before she could say anything, he spun her around until her back faced him, then he began to place kisses over her sensitive skin. With every moan and gasp, he found it harder and harder to remember anything but making love to her.

He knew he was about to pass a barrier in which he had never come to before, and quite frankly, it frightened him more than any creature he had ever faced. For he knew, if he passed that invisible barrier, he might not be able to let Shannon go.

With the pads of his fingers, he traced the line of Shannon's bra until he came to the hook that held it together. He eased his fingers beneath it and unclasped it. The bra fell open, and he pushed the straps from her shoulders and watched the pretty garment fall to the floor.

His gaze traveled down to her narrow waist, then to the exquisite lace of her panties. He turned her back to face him. Her lips were parted, her eyes closed as she allowed him to run his hands over her sleek body.

He hooked his thumbs in her panties and slowly slid them down her legs to pool on the floor. He reached for her, but she shoved his hands aside and pushed him back on the bed. As he watched her, his breath came out in gasps as she pulled off his boots and tossed them to the floor. Next, she began to unlace his trousers and tug them from his body.

His head fell back on the bed. Time stood still as he closed his eyes and let himself feel the wonder of her hands on him. He yearned to have her, but he held off, giving her time to feel his body as he had felt hers.

Her hands skimmed his aching rod, and he nearly came off the bed.

"It's my turn," he heard her whisper as she placed kisses on his chest and abdomen.

He didn't know if he would be able to take it, but he would try. For Shannon.

Her expert hands drove him wild with desire. His blood pounded through his veins, demanding he take her. He gripped the covers to keep his hands from taking hold of her as his passion grew and pulsed within him.

When her hand encircled his rod, he wasn't able to hold back the moan of pleasure that escaped through his clenched teeth. She knew just how and where to touch him to drive him wild. The feel of her soft hair on his thighs as her hands worked their magic only added to his growing lust.

He opened his eyes and met her gaze as she lowered her head, his cock inches from her sweet, heavenly lips.

CHAPTER TWENTY

Shannon had never felt so wanton and free in her life. Holding Cole's thick, hard arousal was exhilarating. It throbbed within her hand as her mouth moved closer to the tip. She ran her fingers along the sleek skin and sighed with pleasure.

She had never touched a man before, never wanted to. But with Cole, everything was different. Her own body pulsed with need as she saw him struggling with the pleasure she gave him.

A bead of liquid pooled at the tip of Cole's rod, and before she could think about it, she leaned over and licked it.

"Shannon," Cole groaned out as his hands bunched up the covers.

She loved her control, and knew it would only last so long before Cole took over.

She ran her tongue along the length of him, enjoying the hiss that escaped through his wonderful lips. But she wanted him to feel more. She wanted to give him the pleasure he always gave her.

With a hand at the base of his cock, she bent down and took him in her mouth. He was hot and tasted salty and exotic. He jerked and issued a long moan, and she began to slide him in and out of her mouth.

She became bolder by the second, taking more of him in her mouth and cupping his sacs with her other hand. He called out her name, his body now thrusting against her.

All of a sudden, she was lifted off of him, and found herself on her knees in front of Cole.

"By the gods, woman, what you do to me," he said just before he claimed her mouth in a scalding kiss that left her breathless.

If he only knew what he did to me.

But she would never tell him. How could she, when she knew she would never see him after tonight? Her body had never, would never, know a better lover, and her heart...her heart would never love as she did at that moment.

Tears filled her eyes as she realized just how much she had come to care for Cole in such a short time. She had never believed in falling in love until it had happened to her. Now, she was faced with leaving the man she loved.

She turned her face away from him as Cole rained kisses down her neck to her breasts. Determined to not let him know how she hurt, she gave in to the desire coursing through her and pushed all else aside.

His magical hands gripped her hips and rubbed his hard rod against her aching sex. She grasped his wide shoulders, pulling him toward her, needing his strength. His head bent and took a nipple into his mouth, suckling until it was a hard, aching nub before he moved to the other nipple.

By the time he was finished with her other breast, her hips rocked against his with need.

"Not yet," he murmured in her ear before he pulled out of her arms.

Shannon reached for him, but he was too quick. When next she felt him, he was behind her. He reached around and took a breast in each hand as he nuzzled her neck.

With his mouth doing delicious things to her neck, one hand tweaking a nipple almost painfully, his other hand dipped down and found her clitoris.

She cried out and dropped her head back onto his shoulder as pleasure ripped through her. He then moved a finger inside of her, matching the rhythm he set as he twirled his thumb over her swollen nub. She was so close to orgasm, just a few more seconds and she would shatter.

Then he stopped.

She started to question him when he pushed her forward onto her hands. She looked back over her shoulder to see him guide his rod into her. She pushed back against him, wanting more, but his hands held her hips in place.

"Please, Cole."

He chuckled softly. "Not yet."

Inch by agonizing inch, Cole entered her. Shannon was panting with need by the time he was fully sheathed. Then he wouldn't move. She was going mad with need, and every time she tried to move, he stopped her.

Suddenly, his hand came around and glided over her aching sex. The spasm of pleasure nearly sent her over the edge, and she prayed he did it again. When he did, it was so fleeting she thought for a moment that she imagined it.

Then he began to move inside of her. She sighed and met his thrusts, climbing higher and higher with each one. His hands moved over her back and bottom all the while.

She cried out as wave upon wave of pleasure washed over her, and as the last of her orgasm ripped through her body she felt Cole give a final thrust before he called out.

They fell as one to the bed. She welcomed his arms as he pulled her back against him. What they had just shared was more special than anything she could have ever imagined. She blinked back the tears that threatened to spill.

"What are you thinking?" she asked.

His hand ran from her shoulder down to her hip. "That, as amazing as you are, it's surprising you haven't already found a husband."

She smiled. "I told you what my life was like in my time. I didn't have time to find a husband."

"Will you now?"

She shook her head. "I think you've spoiled me." She would never admit to him just how much he had spoiled her for other men though. He would forever be in her heart, and she knew that none would ever replace him.

He kissed her shoulder and moved the hair from

her face. "I'm glad we met."

"Me, too."

Cole blinked and slowly sat up.

"What is it?"

"Stay still," he said as he leaned over and examined her arm. His lungs burned, and he realized he was holding his breath. He let loose a breath and ran the pad of his thumb over the back of her arm.

She giggled and looked over her shoulder at him. "What are you doing? I'm ticklish."

"Shannon, do you remember that mark I told you about?"

She nodded, the smile now gone.

"You have it."

"What?" she asked as she turned to face him.

Cole shook his head in disbelieve. "It explains why Gyles brought you here. You are one of the Chosen."

"It doesn't make sense. If I am one of the Chosen, and was brought here for them to kill me, why haven't they?"

Cole shrugged. "Don't question it. You're alive, and we must get you out of here."

Gabriel smiled when he saw Cole and Shannon walk from the dining room. He knew Shannon would keep Cole occupied for several more hours, which gave him all the time he needed to be taken to the castle.

Benton caught his gaze. The tavern keeper was talking to a burly man who kept casting glances at Gabriel. Gabriel fingered the dagger at his waist. He had a feeling they knew what he was, that he was a Shield, which was impossible unless Shannon had told them. He didn't think it was Shannon, though. She wore her feelings on her sleeve, and if she had betrayed them, both he and Cole would have noticed.

Which left only one option.

The evil knew they were here. Gabriel shifted in his chair, looking at each person in the tavern. He was good, but not good enough to take on nearly twenty men single handedly.

He glanced out the window. It was nearly dusk. Another hour or so and all hell would break loose in the village. It was time to get things moving.

Gabriel banged his mug on the table drawing Benton and the other man's attention. "Is there a problem?" he asked casually.

Benton eyed him. "There is."

"Let's take this outside, then," Gabriel said as he rose to his feet and walked around the table toward the door.

He motioned Benton and the other man out before him and followed them to the side of the tavern. "What seems to be the problem? Can strangers not drink in your tavern?"

Benton chuckled. "Strangers can, but you cannot."

"Really?" Gabriel asked, his hands on his hips. "Why is that?"

"We know what you are."

Gabriel froze. His suspicions were right. "What are you referring to?"

"A Shield. That's what we were told you were, you and your friend Cole," Benton said as he pulled his sword from its scabbard. "But we'll take care of you before you mess up our plans."

Gabriel dove and rolled to miss the swing of Benton's sword. As he came to his feet, a meaty fist slammed into his face from the other man. Gabriel staggered back and palmed his dagger in one hand and his sword in the other. How he longed for his bow, but his sword would have to do for now.

He faced both men and wiped away the blood that trickled from his nose and mouth.

"It'll take more than the two of you to take me down."

His blood froze in his veins when Benton laughed.

"We know," Benton said as he and the other man advanced on him at once.

"What was that?" Cole asked as he sat up.

Shannon sat up with him and listened. "What?"

"You don't hear it?"

She shook her head.

But Cole had. It was the unmistakable sound of swords. Someone was fighting, and he knew who it was. His head swung to Shannon. "He asked you to keep me occupied didn't he?"

When Shannon refused to meet his gaze he had his answer. He jumped off the bed and began to pull on his clothes.

"Don't be angry with him, Cole. We were only looking out for you."

He stopped and looked at her. "I know. Get

dressed. It's time to get you out of here."

Cole finished with his clothes and grabbed his weapons. When he turned back to Shannon, she stood by the door waiting for him.

"Ready?"

"No," she said and ran into his arms. She held him tightly as if she were afraid to let him go.

He squeezed his eyes shut as he breathed in her scent. "Soon you'll be away from this madness."

"But also away from you."

He pulled back and looked into her eyes. He had been afraid she might bring up what had happened between them, and it was because he didn't have an answer that he didn't wish to talk about it. Not yet. "Shannon…"

"I know," she interrupted him. "Just promise me you'll be careful."

"Always." He waited for her to nod that she was ready, and then he unbarred her door and opened it.

To find the giant that had been with Gyles.

Cole instantly palmed his double-headed war axe and faced the big man. "Run," he yelled at Shannon.

Shannon opened her mouth to scream as Cole raised his massive war axe over his head and swung it at the giant before him. She backed away, hearing his words, but not registering them.

"Shannon. Now," he bellowed as he ducked, the slice of a sword barely missing his neck.

She swallowed and looked around her tiny room. The only way out was through the door, but Cole and the giant blocked her way. Then she caught sight of the window.

She jerked up her skirts and climbed onto the ledge. With one last look at Cole, she dropped to the ground outside.

The woods were just a few feet away. She could make it there and wait for Cole. She took a step toward the dense trees and came to an abrupt halt as castle guards surrounded her.

CHAPTER TWENTY-ONE

Cole turned his attention to the huge man before him. Now that Shannon was safe he could find Gabriel.

Cole didn't waste any time attacking the guard. Giant or not, he was just a man, and all men had their weaknesses. His was that he moved too slowly. Cole was able to dash around him and lead him into the dining room, all the while ducking and sidestepping the giant's swings and thrusts.

Just as Cole was just about to deliver his final swing, the big man suddenly rushed him, sending both of them into the heavy wooden door. Cole grunted as the weight of the man slammed him into the door, which gave a loud creak and crashed to the ground with a bone jarring thud.

He was sure he heard some bones break under the immense weight of the giant, but didn't have time to take stock of his injuries. The giant reared up and sent a meaty fist into Cole's jaw. Pain exploded through his head. Before another punch landed, Cole moved his hand to reach for the dagger he kept at his waist.

Cole opened his eyes in time to see the fist coming at him. He tried to move his head, but only managed to deflect the punch from his nose to his eye. He knew if he didn't do something soon, the giant would render him unconscious.

He gnashed his teeth and yanked the dagger from its sheath, and then with a vicious thrust, embedded the blade in the giant's neck. The man's eyes bugged from his head as blood gushed from the wound. Then the giant slumped forward.

Cole let out a long string of curses as he worked to get the huge man off him. By the time he was done, he could hardly open his mouth, and his eye had swollen shut. He climbed to his feet and grabbed his axe.

He was about to make a run for the trees when he spotted Gabriel and Benton. Cole sheathed his war axe at his back and unhooked the two smaller axes at his waist. He walked toward Gabriel and Benton, his anger growing with each step he took.

"Cole," Gabriel said as he approached.

"Benton is mine," Cole answered, never taking his eyes off him. Out of the corner of his good eye, he saw Gabriel nod and turn to another guard who attacked.

"I'm surprised to find you still alive," Benton said as they circled each other.

Cole clenched his jaw. "As I am with you. I assumed you would have run off as soon as you found out you weren't going to live."

Benton laughed. "We know who you are. Shields. Now, when I expected to have the legendary Shields come to my village, I assumed they would be men who would put fear in us. Instead, they sent you."

"At least now you'll pick on someone your own size. I've been waiting for this moment since the first night I saw you."

Benton smiled. "You'll never win."

Cole lunged at him, one arm bringing the axe over his head, while the other arm swung from the side toward Benton. His axe overhead stopped Benton's sword and gave him just the time he needed to embed the other axe in Benton's side.

"The Shields always win," he said as he pushed Benton's dying form to the ground.

He stood over the man who had held Shannon captive and abused her, and he wanted to kill him all over again. Once just wasn't enough.

"Cole!"

He jerked and spun toward Gabriel who was surrounded by castle guards. Cole rushed to help his friend, and soon found himself in the thick of battle.

There was no time to do anything but stay alive and kill as many of the guards as they could. Cole and Gabriel stood back to back, each watching out for the other.

It was some time later before he and Gabriel realized the last man had been killed. They surveyed the carnage around them with grim satisfaction.

"Are you injured?" Gabriel asked.

"My eye is swollen and my jaw feels like it's on fire."

"Anything else?"

Cole didn't want to think of himself right now. He

needed to find Shannon and get her out of there before Gyles came looking for them.

"They know who we are."

"I know," Gabriel said and shifted to face him. "I just don't understand why they didn't capture us. It was as if they wanted a fight. As if they wanted our attention turned."

Cole felt as though someone kicked him in the stomach. Without a backward glance, he ran into the forest, screaming Shannon's name. He heard footfalls behind him and knew Gabriel followed.

He crashed through the forest, not caring who, or what, might be lying in wait for him. Never had Cole been so terrified. He came a halt when he saw Aimery waiting for him.

"Do you have her?" he asked the Fae commander between mouthfuls of air.

Aimery shook his head. "I felt your...emotions...and came at once. It didn't take long to discover they have her at the castle. I take it she's one of the women?"

Cole nodded numbly. "I just discovered it tonight. I never expected them to take her."

"They wanted us otherwise engaged so they could," Gabriel said as he leaned against a tree to get his breath back. "I never saw it coming."

"And you wouldn't have been able to," Aimery said. "You know the situation, now do what you have to do."

Cole glanced at Gabriel. "We go to the castle."

"Oh, aye," Gabriel agreed and pushed away from the tree. "I need to tend to you."

"Nay. There isn't time," Cole stated. "I have to get

Shannon back."

Gabriel waved his words. "Let's go then."

Cole turned to Aimery. "Keep her alive."

He didn't wait for Aimery to respond, but hastened after Gabriel.

Aimery watched them race towards the castle. Every fiber of his being yearned to go with them, to fight the evil that raged inside the castle walls.

But he was forbidden.

Suddenly, he smiled. He might not be able to fight alongside the Shields, but he could help in other ways.

Shannon huddled in a ball in the dark, dank room. She was going to die. She knew it as surely as she knew she loved Cole. She still couldn't believe she hadn't escaped the guards, nevermind that there had been ten of them surrounding her.

Her fear kept her shaking, her mind frozen in disbelief. Where was Cole? Had he been killed? Taken prisoner? Those were the only explanations as to why he hadn't come for her. He had given her his word, and only death would keep him from keeping it.

But she refused to believe he was dead. Injured he might be, but Gabriel would be able to heal him. He had healed the black magic that nearly took Cole.

She tried to think of the many reasons Cole hadn't come, but none of it made a difference. He and Gabriel had tried their best to keep her safe, and if they had known earlier she was one of the Chosen, she wouldn't be in this predicament.

Tears stung the back of her eyes, but she refused to give in. How many times in her life had it looked like she was down for the count? Many, and yet every time she had managed to scrape through using her wits and resources.

But this wasn't the twenty-first century. This was Medieval England, and she didn't know what resources to use. Gyles and whatever evil was out there wanted her dead. They had gone to great lengths to ensure her death, and nothing short of a miracle was going to save her now.

She put her head down on her knees and let the tears flow. The only regret she had was not telling Cole she loved him. It wouldn't have changed anything, but she would have at least let him know how he had changed her life.

The sound of boot heels against the stone floor reached her. Someone was coming.

Cole and Gabriel approached the castle gate, ready to scale it if needed. No sooner had they reached it than the chains rattled as the gate opened.

They exchanged a glance and palmed their weapons. Gabriel readied his bow, and Cole let his two axes hang by his side.

"No guards," Gabriel whispered.

"They're here. They're just not showing themselves, but I can feel their gazes."

Cole and Gabriel walked through the gate into the bailey, turning and looking around them to ensure no one tried to sneak up behind them. Once they were through the gate, it closed with a loud bang, signaling finality.

Cole stared at the gate a moment before he lifted his gaze to the castle. Shannon was somewhere inside, and he was determined to find her.

"Lay down your weapons," a voice ordered.

Cole and Gabriel both searched the castle and surrounding battlements but found no one.

"It's another trap," Gabriel warned.

Cole chuckled. "Of course it is, but this time we're prepared."

As soon as they lay down their weapons, guards surrounded them. Cole didn't flinch as the tips of swords jabbed into his skin. They might make him feel pain now, but it was nothing to what he would do to them once he found Shannon.

"Here are the rules," an older man said as he stepped forward through the guards.

"You'll be put into the maze separately. 'Tis up to you to find your way out before the beast finds you."

Cole glared at the older man, clearly the steward of Gyles'. "I suppose we go weaponless."

"Of course," the man said with a smile that didn't reach his eyes. "We want you to die, not kill the beast."

"What beast is it you hold?" Gabriel asked.

The man cackled, his bald head shining in the moonlight. "You will discover that soon enough."

Cole was grabbed and shoved toward the castle. He gave Gabriel a look, they knew what they had to do, and they would make sure it was done, weapons or not. There wasn't time to share words as the guards took Cole one way and Gabriel another.

Cole made sure to recall everything to memory as he was rushed through the great hall, and down a long dark hallway to stand before another gate, this one half the size of the castle gate. His heart thumped almost painfully as he readied himself to discover what creature waited.

The door opened and mist swirled through the opening to hang on to Cole like a damp cloak. He lifted his foot to step through the gate when the steward's voice stopped him.

"Oh. I almost forgot to tell you, the wench is already inside. Of course, the beast may have already gotten to her by now. Either way, you're all dead by dawn."

Rage erupted in Cole, and he lunged at the steward, but the guards shoved him through the doorway and closed the gate. He clenched his hands and turned to face the maze.

Thick, dark gray stone walls stood before him. Night had fallen, leaving only the stars and moon as a guide. Cole stood and listened, hoping he would hear either Shannon or the beast, but he heard only silence.

"At least this creature doesn't fly," he mumbled to himself as he turned to the right.

The door creaked open, and Shannon found herself staring at Gyles, his sinister smile brought bile to her throat.

"Did you honestly believe you would escape?" he

asked as he shut the door and walked towards her. "After all the trouble we went through to bring you here, did you think we would allow you to leave?"

Frankly, Shannon didn't give a damn what he thought. She shrugged and watched as he squatted in front of her.

"You're going to die. Tonight," he said, a smirk on his face.

The first time she had seen him she had thought him sort of attractive. He wasn't short or tall, just average, his build was average and his blonde hair and blue eyes looked good at first glance. Then she got to see his creepy personality and recognized him for the evil that he was. No amount of fair looks could hide that.

"People like you always get their comeuppance."

He threw back his head and laughed. "Not people with the power I have. Do you know exactly what I have in the maze?"

She was almost afraid to ask, but maybe if she found out she could tell Cole.

"What?"

"A minotaur. A fearsome beast twice the size of a man with strength that could crush your skull with his bare hands," he said as he lifted a hand and fisted it. "Horns that will gullet you with one swipe, and hooves for feet that will smash every bone in your body with one kick. He feeds on human flesh."

"I suppose I'm to be his meal tonight." She tried to sound brave, but it came out as a squeak.

Gyles smiled and pulled a strand of her hair through his fingers. "Aye, but as of this moment, he is about to dine on two of your friends."

Shannon felt all the blood drain from her face and pool at her feet. "No," she whispered. Surely Cole would never go into the maze, not knowing what he faced.

"Oh, I'm quite sure of it. Saw my men put both Cole and Gabriel into the maze." He laughed as he rose to his feet. "They think they are going in to save you."

Shannon couldn't believe her ears. "Why? You already have me."

"Aye, I do," he said as he stopped and leaned against the door. "I also know who Cole and Gabriel are. They are here to kill the minotaur and destroy the stone that gives me power. I cannot – and will not – allow that to happen."

"You're a monster, and if Cole and Gabriel fail, there will be more Shields sent."

Gyles ran a finger along his chin. "Probably, but then I'll have killed one of the women needed to terminate the evil threatening this realm."

She closed her eyes and fought back more tears. She would not allow him to see how frightened she was, not just for herself but for Cole, Gabriel, and Earth.

"Why would you want to destroy your own realm?" she asked him.

He shrugged. "Why not? What has it brought me? Besides, my loyalty to the Master will be rewarded."

Shannon had heard enough. She rose on shaking legs and faced him. "Get it over with. I'm tired of hearing your talk."

She thought he might laugh at her and tell her more tidbits. Instead, he pulled out his sword as the smile dropped from his face. But she wouldn't back down now. Cole and Gabriel faced impossible odds and did it with courage. She could at least attempt to do the same.

Gyles raised his sword, his eyes glittering in anticipation. But before he could swing the mighty weapon, a bright light flashed in the room, nearly blinding them.

Shannon brought her arm up to shield her eyes and found a dagger about a foot in length with a wickedly curved blade in her hand.

She looked to her left and spotted a man so gorgeous he couldn't possibly be real smiling at her. His long white blond hair fell down his back, but it were his amazing blue eyes that held her captive. Her gaze shifted back to Gyles to find his eyes widening and his mouth hanging open as he stared.

"You won't stop me," he shouted as he lunged at Shannon.

But she had been ready for him. She ducked and pivoted and brought the dagger up and over her shoulder. The sickening feel of her blade sinking into skin met her arm.

She refused to look at Gyles. Instead, she loosened her hold on the dagger and straightened.

She kept her gaze on the man who had suddenly appeared in the room, afraid that if she saw what she had done she would crumble. Especially since she held onto her calm by a very thin thread.

"He's dead."

She nodded. "Who are you?"

"I'm Aimery, commander of the Shields and the Fae army."

Shannon lowered her gaze and sighed. "I've never killed anyone before."

She felt more than saw Aimery move toward her. "You didn't have a choice. Now," he said and raised her chin with his finger. "We have to hurry."

They had just reached the door when they heard the roar.

CHAPTER TWENTY-TWO

Cole ran through the maze calling out for Shannon. With every turn he rounded, he just knew he would find her.

"Shannon! I'm coming. Just hold on for me, sweetheart!" he yelled. If nothing else, she would hear him and know he hadn't abandoned her.

The crunching of footsteps behind him drew Cole up against a stone wall to wait. He had no doubt it was the creature. He hadn't been quiet, he had been hollering for Shannon since the moment he entered the maze.

He readied himself to kill so he could concentrate on finding and freeing Shannon. When Gabriel stepped around the corner, Cole was more than a little surprised.

"You found me?"

Gabriel raised an eyebrow and shook his head. "Everyone on this realm could hear you shouting for your woman. I just followed your voice."

Cole raked a hand through his hair and leaned his head against the stone. "Have you seen the creature?"

"Nay, and that disturbs me."

At that moment, they heard the awesome roar. Cole grabbed Gabriel by his leather vest. "Have you seen Shannon?"

Gabriel shook his head. "I don't think she's in here."

"She has to be here," Cole ground out and turned away from Gabriel. "Creature! I'm here. Come and get me!" he bellowed.

He heard Gabriel curse and hoped his friend understood that he had no other choice. To face the creature was to find out what had happened to Shannon.

Yet, with each moment that ticked by and the creature didn't come forward, the more Cole worried.

"I don't think the creature is in the maze either."

Cole stared at Gabriel, afraid to admit he was right. "If neither Shannon nor the creature is in the maze, then why are we here?"

"It's time we leave," Gabriel said as he turned and began to climb the walls.

Cole quickly followed and rose to stand beside Gabriel atop the wall. From their vantage point they could see the entire maze. It didn't take them long to discover they were alone.

"There," Gabriel said and pointed.

He followed Gabriel's gaze and found an area on the outside of the castle they could scale to get them inside. In the next instant, he bent so his fingers found a hold, and he began his climb with Gabriel below and to the right of him.

Cole's eye was now fully closed, giving him a limited view of his surroundings. His arms shook, and he was beginning to think he had passed the window Gabriel had pointed out.

"To your left," Gabriel called.

Cole turned his head all the way to the left and was just able to make out the window they could climb through. As he scooted toward the window he heard shouts from the village and turned to find many of the homes burning.

"By the gods," Gabriel cursed. "The creature. He's there."

"Faster," Cole urged. He had to find Shannon, had to know she was alive.

His fingers closed on the windowsill, and he hoisted himself up and through the small window to land with a thud on the hard stone floor. His injured bones protested, and he groaned as he rolled to his side and came up on his feet.

"You're injured worse than you said," Gabriel said as he jumped through the window.

"I'll heal. Shannon won't," Cole said as he raced to the door.

"Give me a moment to tend you," Gabriel argued.

Cole spun around and glared at his friend. "I don't have a moment."

"And how will you explain to Shannon that you couldn't save her because you were too weak?"

Cole hated when Gabriel was right. "Let's search the castle. If she isn't here I'll let you heal me, but you have only a little time. I can't allow the town to be massacred because I was more worried about myself."

"I'll meet you in the great hall then," Gabriel said and threw open the door and ran to the left.

Cole ventured right, calling for Shannon as he went. He was just about to give up when he heard his name.

"Cole. I'm here!"

He looked down from the balcony on the third floor to see Shannon in the great hall. Her brilliant smile was like a beacon. He quickly rushed down the stairs to her.

Just the sight of her sent his heart racing. He threw open his arms and she ran into them. As he enveloped her, he knew he could no longer deny just how precious she had come to be to him.

"Shannon, there is something I have to tell you," he said into her dark tresses.

"Not now," Aimery said as he walked up with Gabriel. "Time is of the essence."

Cole loosened his hold on Shannon and looked from her to Aimery. "What happened?"

"I killed Gyles," Shannon said softly.

Aimery nodded. "I just happened to be in the chamber and gave her the weapon with which to do it."

Cole smiled at Aimery. "Thank you."

"My pleasure."

Gabriel nodded. "And with Gyles dead, the creature is free to kill at will."

"The minotaur," Shannon corrected. "You'll be facing a minotaur."

Cole gave her a quick kiss. "Stay here. Gabriel and I

will take care of this."

"No."

"Please," he begged her. "Look for the stone while we battle the minotaur. It will take both me and Gabriel to kill this creature."

He knew she wanted to argue, but she quietly agreed.

Cole raised his gaze to Aimery. "Can you stay with her?"

"I'll stay for as long as I am able."

Cole gave her a smile that he hoped portrayed his feelings, and followed Gabriel from the castle.

Shannon watched Cole leave. Again. She didn't like the sick feeling in her stomach. Cole might be immortal, but the injuries to his face were enough to let her know that he could be hurt and he was in pain.

"He'll heal quickly," Aimery said from beside her.

"He's immortal. Of course, he will." She took a deep breath and faced the Fae.

"I never thanked you for helping me."

He shrugged and gave her a bright smile. "I always did like to break the rules every now and again. Shall we look for the stone?"

"Yes," Shannon said. Before she turned away, Aimery stopped her and handed her the dagger she had used to kill Gyles.

"You might need this."

She nodded and tied the dagger, now sheathed, around her waist. "I just might."

~ ~ ~

Cole and Gabriel reached the village to see people screaming and running for their lives. Through the smoke of the fires, they spotted the minotaur, his massive form striking at anyone who got near.

Gabriel pointed to the right. Cole nodded and slipped off to the left. They would circle the creature and corner him, then kill him. It was a simple plan, a plan that would have worked had the child not gotten in the way.

Cole spotted the toddler screaming in the road the same time the minotaur did. The minotaur let out a roar and rushed for the child. Cole took aim and released an axe that embedded in the minotaur's back just as he reached the child. It gave Cole the moment he needed to grab the toddler and hand him to a woman who he urged to race to the forest.

No sooner had he handed the child off than he was yanked backwards to land with a jaw jarring thud that knocked the air from his lungs. As he struggled for breath, the minotaur loomed over him.

"I've been waiting for you," the beast growled before he lifted his hand, ready to strike.

Cole didn't think, he just reacted. He immediately rolled away and came to his feet, reaching for his axe. But his hand came up empty. He scanned the area and found his double-headed war axe several paces away and closed his hand on the pommel of his sword.

He studied the minotaur as the creature slowly advanced. "You weren't in the maze."

The creature laughed. "I was there and ready to

strike when I was released with the death of Gyles."

"I'd have thought the killing of Shields would have overruled your need to slaughter the village."

"I knew you'd come. You Shields always do."

Out of the corner of his eye, Cole saw Gabriel approach. He unsheathed his sword and circled the creature. "Your time is at an end."

In response, the minotaur roared and lunged at him. Cole spun and brought his sword around to slash the creature's chest. Bright red bubbled and fell from the open wound, but it healed just as quickly.

The minotaur advanced, his great arms swinging in an attempt to get hold of Cole. Cole used his quick feet to keep out of the way. Several glancing blows caught him, and the strength of the minotaur gave him pause.

While Cole kept the minotaur occupied, Gabriel had taken aim and let loose a flurry of arrows. The creature screamed in pain and turned to Gabriel. Cole used the chance to dive for his axe.

He gained his feet to see that the minotaur had Gabriel by the neck squeezing the life from him. Cole's blood rushed in his ears. He ran towards the creature, his axe lifted over his head.

The minotaur raised his arm, his claws unsheathed. Cole had just enough time to reach him before he struck Gabriel with a killing blow. Using all his power, Cole swung the axe at the minotaur's arm and heard the slice of the blade as it connected and the creature's hand fell to the earth.

The momentum of Cole's swing brought him forward, and he rolled to land on his feet. When he turned around, he found Gabriel on the ground and the minotaur holding his arm against his chest. The roar the creature issued sent chills of dread racing down Cole's back.

Before he could blink, the minotaur raced toward the castle. Cole helped Gabriel to his feet, both men staring at the destruction and death the creature wrought.

"How does your neck feel?" Cole asked.

Gabriel shrugged. "Probably as good as your swollen eye," he said, his voice cracking and hoarse.

"We'll mend later. Let's kill this thing."

CHAPTER TWENTY-THREE

Cole and Gabriel raced through the open gates of the castle. What few guards they found were slaughtered, which left the castle empty except for Shannon, Aimery, and the minotaur.

"He went to the maze," Gabriel said.

Cole nodded. "It's his home. Let's find Shannon and Aimery first to see if they have the stone. It won't be long before the creature has his hand back."

They ran into the castle and found Shannon and Aimery searching Gyles' chamber. Shannon looked up as they entered, a welcoming smile on her face.

"Both of you look like hell. Did you kill it?"

Cole grinned. "Nay. We wounded him, but it's just a matter of time before he attacks again."

"Did you find the stone?" Gabriel asked.

Aimery shook his head. "The most logical place would be in this chamber, yet we haven't found it."

"It's here," Cole said. "Gyles wouldn't have put it too far away."

"I agree," Aimery said.

As one, all four left the chamber and walked to the hallway.

"Gabriel and I should keep an eye on the minotaur. Be ready to strike before he fully heals," Cole said.

"Good idea," Aimery said and looked to Shannon. "I'm being called back. I can't stay. You're going to have to find the stone."

Shannon nodded woodenly. She had never felt so much pressure in her life. From what Aimery had told her while they searched Gyles chamber, the creatures were near invincible. Each one had a certain way to kill it, and the most effective way was by smashing the blue stone.

Her gaze turned to Cole. He looked a mess, and she wanted nothing more than to hold him tightly against her. "I'll find it," she promised.

He stepped toward her and brought her into his arms. "I know," he said just before he kissed her.

The kiss was slow, soft, but it held something in it that she hadn't felt before. Something she dared not ask him about until the creature was dead.

"Whatever happens, stay out of the minotaur's way," Cole warned. "If we fail – "

"You won't," she interrupted.

He smiled sadly. "If we fail, stay hidden and call to Aimery. He'll see you safe."

Shannon glanced at Aimery to see the Fae smile at her before he disappeared before her eyes. She turned back to Cole. "I…"

"I know," he said and kissed her forehead. "Remember what I told you."

She nodded and clenched her hands in an effort to not drag him back to her as he walked away. He stopped just before he reached the stairs and turned to her. She was barely able to make out his face in the dimly lit hallway, but she thought she saw him smile. She returned his wave, and then he was gone.

Shannon leaned against the stone wall and wondered where she should search next. The castle was huge, with many rooms and corridors. It would take her weeks, if not months, to search every room.

She looked back into Gyles' room. She was sure they would find the stone there. Her feet took her back into the room. Something told her to look again. The trunk against the wall caught her attention. She had searched it, dumping the entire contents on the floor. But maybe she missed something.

Aimery took a deep breath before walking into the throne room. Theron and Rufina awaited him, and it wasn't until he was nearly before them that he noticed they were alone.

"Aimery," Rufina said in a choked voice. "What have you done?"

Theron glanced at his wife before he stood and walked down the steps to Aimery.

"You've brought attention to us. I know you needed to help Shannon, but giving her one of our weapons to kill Gyles goes against what we are allowed to do."

Aimery had been prepared for this. "We just gave Mina and Elle weapons to help kill the harpies. This isn't so different."

"I know," Theron said with a loud sigh. "The evil is one step ahead of us. We'll never defeat him unless we can outmaneuver him."

"I have reports from my army that the sightings of creatures have dwindled."

"What?" Rufina asked as she rose to her feet. "How is that possible?"

"Think about it, love," Theron said and reached for his wife's hand. "The evil discovered information about the Chosen Ones. He now realizes that they will determine if his plans succeed."

Aimery nodded in agreement. "He's focusing all his efforts on finding the other two Chosen Ones and killing them."

"Aimery –"

"I've already dispatched my army, sire. They'll find where the other two creatures have surfaced."

Rufina shook her head sadly. "Let us pray that we reach the Chosen Ones before the evil does."

Cole and Gabriel overlooked the maze from the castle window they climbed through earlier. They could hear the creature as he continued to bellow in pain, but they hadn't yet found him.

"I don't see him," Gabriel said.

Cole shook his head. "Me either. He must be

hiding."

"Where did he enter?" Gabriel asked. "I was brought to the maze at the back, near the bailey."

"I was brought in through the castle. My guess is that he went the same way you were brought. Quicker and easier than trying to go through the castle."

Gabriel nodded. "I'll move there and watch the entrance."

"Stay safe."

With one last look, Gabriel turned and disappeared down the hallway. Cole went down on his haunches and prayed for the clouds to move away from the moon so he could have more light. If he could get a view of the creature, he could attempt to wound him again. As it was, the clouds were many and left him little to no light to see by.

He decided to walk the top of the maze as he and Gabriel had done when they escaped. He blinked his bad eye, noting that the swelling had gone down somewhat, but it still hindered his ability to see clearly. He would have to rely on his hearing to make up for his eye.

With a quick adjustment of his sword and axes, he jumped from the window and landed on a thick wall of the maze. "Time for some hunting," he whispered as he unsheathed his doubled-headed axe.

Shannon threw the clothes down with a vicious snarl. How could she have been so wrong? She had wasted precious time looking in a chest that had already been searched. Suddenly, the roars of the minotaur reverberated throughout the castle, sending ice through her veins as panic began to choke her.

Her fear for Cole and Gabriel grew with each second that passed. She jumped to her feet and slipped on what she thought was a tunic. As she moved her foot, she saw the parchment. She hurriedly unrolled it to see a language she didn't understand, but she was able to make out the crudely drawn map.

"Oh, my God. It's a map to the stone," she whispered. She clutched the map in her hand and scrambled to her feet. In her haste to leave the chamber, she fell as she rounded the corner into the hallway.

Her heart pounded in her chest, and her blood rushed in her ears. She couldn't shake the unmistakable knowledge that she wouldn't get to Cole in time.

She stopped in the great hall, unsure of how to get to the maze. She turned, grabbed up the hated skirts and sprinted out of the castle into the bailey. The minotaur's roars had lessened, which meant her time was running out.

In her mind, she imagined an alarm clock with only seconds before the alarm sounded and all was lost.

Her gaze swept the bailey. It was completely deserted and quiet as a tomb. She began to run across the bailey when she saw movement to her left. Her head turned, and she spotted Gabriel and turned midstride toward him.

"I found a map," she said. "A map to the stone."

His brow furrowed. "What kind of fool would leave a map to the stone?"

"This kind of fool," she said and held up the map.

Gabriel looked it over and cursed. "Come on," he said and took her arm as he dragged her to the castle wall.

To her surprise, she saw an entrance that would otherwise have been hidden. Gabriel hastened through it, and she followed, trusting him completely.

She stared in horror at the massive walls that surrounded her. Solving puzzles had always been a specialty she had, but now, she was beginning to hate them.

"The maze."

"Aye. Stay near me," he warned.

"Where is Cole?"

"Somewhere in the maze," he whispered over his shoulder.

"We'll find him."

Shannon's entire body shook with fear. She compared it to the insane times she went with friends during Halloween to the old buildings they converted to haunted houses.

She was never one who liked the thrill of the scare. Safe and secure, that was Shannon.

The minotaur's roars ceased altogether. She reached up and took hold of Gabriel's vest. He turned and looked at her, but all she could do was shrug. How could she tell him that all the horror movies she watched had the person who was last taken first?

Instead of blurting that fact out, she kept hold of his leather vest and constantly looked over her shoulder to see if anything had snuck up behind her.

CHAPTER TWENTY-FOUR

Cole ceased his movements on the top of the maze when the minotaur's roars stopped. He waited expectantly, but when no more roars ensued, he knew the minotaur had fully healed.

Slowly, he squatted and closed his eyes as he opened his ears to the sounds around him. If he concentrated hard enough he would be able to pick up the movements of the creature.

Several heartbeats passed before he heard the heavy footfalls of the creature to the front and left of him. He was about to stand when he heard something else. Two more sets of footfalls. One long, and one short and quick.

His eyes flew open.

Shannon!

He knew Gabriel would have had to have a very good reason for bringing Shannon this close to the creature, but it still didn't stop the anger that consumed him. Gabriel and Shannon were to his right and slowly coming towards him, just as the creature was. He had to get to them before the creature did.

Cole sprang up and jumped from wall to wall as he hurried. He never looked down, only concentrated on finding Shannon. The scene in his dream where he held Shannon's dead body flashed in his mind, and he realized just where he had been while holding her.

The maze.

He refused to allow the dream to come to pass. He'd sacrifice his own life for hers. It wasn't simply because she was one of the women chosen to aid Earth, but because he loved her. Aye, the gods help him, he loved her.

Finally, he saw them. With one final leap to his right, he dropped down behind them.

Gabriel spun around, his sword ready to strike, but Cole's eyes were for Shannon. She took one look at him and flew into his arms. He allowed himself a heartbeat to hold her tight before he pulled away.

He looked over her head to Gabriel and motioned that the creature was headed toward them. Cole placed a finger over Shannon's lips to keep her quiet.

In response, she held up a piece of parchment. He unrolled it but wasn't able to discern much with the clouds covering the moonlight.

With a shrug, he handed her the parchment.

She pulled him down and moved her mouth by his ear. "This is where the stone is."

He jerked back not believing her words until Gabriel nodded. Cole raked a hand through his hair. He took her hands in his and gave her a squeeze.

"Go with Gabriel. Find the stone and smash it," he

whispered.

"And you?"

"I'll keep the creature occupied." He glanced at Gabriel to make sure he heard.

"Come," Gabriel whispered and took Shannon's arm.

Cole didn't want to let her go. He couldn't shake the picture of her dead body out of his mind. When they rounded the corner and she was out of sight, he readied his axe and walked toward the creature.

"Looking for me?" Cole shouted. "I could hear your heavy breathing in another realm. I would've thought this great evil, your Master, would have chosen a more competent creature to try and best the Shields," he taunted.

And just as he expected, he heard the loud snort and the pawing of hooves as the minotaur readied to strike.

Shannon had seen the resolution in Cole's handsome face. He thought he was going to die. Well, she wasn't about to let that happen, not when she had the means to end it all.

"Hurry," she urged Gabriel.

He threw her an annoyed look over his shoulder as he began to jog through the maze. She banged her shoulder against a stone wall as they turned sharply and winced as the pain lanced through her.

"I hope you know where you're going," she mumbled.

If Gabriel heard her, he chose not to respond and instead lengthened his stride.

Shannon was now in a full out run to keep up with him. Her breath burned her lungs and a stitch started in her side.

She bit her lip when she heard Cole taunting the minotaur. He shouldn't be out there alone. She had yet to see the creature, but from Gyles' description, he would be terrifying.

Gabriel halted, and she took that time to look at the map again. She had to squint to see through the dim light the moon poured through the dense clouds.

"What I wouldn't do for a flashlight."

"What?" Gabriel asked.

She shook her head. "Nothing. If you can get me to the main entrance, I think I can find this."

Gabriel cleared his throat, and she looked up to see his arms crossed over his chest. She looked around him and saw the great door behind him.

"Oh," she said and turned to face the maze. "We need to go left then venture back towards the center."

"This will take us near the creature."

She shrugged. "I didn't put the stone there, Gabriel. Now, come on," she said and took off. Her fear had been displaced by worry for Cole.

Gabriel soon took the lead, and she was grateful for it. She had no idea where she was going, but thankfully Gabriel did. It didn't cross her mind to question him. She knew his need to find the stone was greater than hers.

She was just about to think she read the map wrong when Gabriel stopped again. He stared at the wall, and she came to stand beside him to see what he looked at.

"The stone," she said in awe as it twinkled blue in the overshadowed light of the moon.

Immediately Gabriel reached for it. But no matter how hard he pulled and tugged, the stone wouldn't budge. He cursed in a language she had never heard before and used both hands, but it never moved.

Cole leaned against the stone wall and waited. It didn't take the creature long to find him. "How's the arm?" Cole asked.

The minotaur's eyes blazed red in their fury. "You'll pay for that."

Cole saw the creature shift a second before he charged, and he sidestepped and brought up his massive axe, ready to cleave off another limb as the creature got close enough. Cole chuckled as the minotaur circled him, but didn't allow himself to get within arm's length of him.

The creature snorted and growled. This time when he charged, he lowered his head. Cole swung his axe at the minotaur's legs as he rolled out of the way. He heard the satisfying sound of his blade sinking into flesh.

His satisfaction was quickly dimmed as a burning pain in his side got his attention as he stood. He looked down to see a gash from his back to his ribs.

He looked up at the minotaur and saw him smile. "That's the only piece of me you'll get," Cole said as he shifted his stance.

The minotaur lashed at Cole with his long arms and vicious claws. Cole ducked, but with his bad eye, he never saw the blow to his left side.

Gabriel stopped trying to work the stone free. Shannon pushed him over and tried to wedge her fingers between the rock and the blue stone until they bled. It wasn't until she lowered her hand that she noticed something in the stone. She ran her sore fingers over it as she examined it.

"We need a key," she mumbled. She turned to Gabriel. "Did you hear me?"

"Shhh," he said and held up his hand.

They stood in silence for several minutes as she waited for him to do something.

"He's in trouble," Gabriel suddenly said.

She knew without being told he meant Cole. "Go to him. I'll keep trying to get the stone out."

As Gabriel disappeared in the maze, Shannon fingered the dagger at her side. It would be useless against the minotaur, but at least she had some defense.

She turned back to the stone and pulled her dagger from the sheath. She tried in vain to insert it where the key would go to release the stone.

Then she tried to use the blade to dislodge the stone. Several times she thought she might have managed to make progress, only to have the blade slip out.

Her frustration grew until she was trembling with it. "Please," she cried out.

Cole forced his hands to move and push himself up. He had lost track of how many times he was slashed with the creature's mighty claws. There might have been even more cuts from his horns, but he wasn't sure.

The pain had been so great on his already bruised and battered body that he lost consciousness at least once while the creature pummeled him. He was exhausted and barely able to move, but he did make out the grunts coming from his left.

Cole raised his head to see Gabriel. His first thought was of Shannon. He looked around for her but didn't find her. His only hope was that Gabriel had left her somewhere safe.

There was no doubt in Cole's mind that Gabriel had gotten there just in time. Cole blinked and tried to rise as the minotaur slammed Gabriel up against the wall.

He winced as Gabriel's head hit the stone.

Focusing all his strength on pulling himself up, he missed Gabriel freeing himself. When Cole next looked up, Gabriel stood fighting the beast. Cole took a deep breath and bent to retrieve his axe.

Already, his wounds had begun to heal, but he couldn't wait for them to finish. Gabriel needed help. He pushed off the wall and moved to the back of the minotaur. He gripped his sword with both hands before he raised it over his head and swung it toward the beast.

The blow wasn't as forceful as usual, but it was enough to turn the minotaur's attention from Gabriel to him.

"I thought you were dead," the minotaur roared.

Cole shrugged and leaned his hip against the wall for support. "I'm rather hard to kill."

"Then I'll have to make sure you're dead this time."

Cole watched as the minotaur reared back to strike him, but before the beast swung his arm, an arrow pierced him in the forearm. As the minotaur roared and pulled the arrow from his arm, Cole and Gabriel exchanged a smile.

Together, Cole and Gabriel began to attack the minotaur, but not even their Fae crafted weapons had much of an impact on the creature. Suddenly, the minotaur threw back his arm and hit Gabriel. Cole watched Gabriel slam into the ground just a moment before the minotaur kicked out his hoof and connected with Cole's abdomen.

Cole tried to take a breath and knew he had at least one rib broken. He took shallow breaths and was slowly picking himself up when he heard Shannon's cry. His gaze jerked to Gabriel and he saw a sliver of fear in Gabriel's silver eyes. Cole then turned to the minotaur, only to find the beast rushing towards the sound of Shannon's scream.

"Nay," Cole said and stumbled to his feet, the pain forgotten. He bent and retrieved his war axe and chased after the creature.

"This way," Gabriel said as he caught up with him.

When they rounded the corner and saw the minotaur towering over Shannon, Cole tasted real horror.

"Fight me," he yelled and threw one of his smaller axes. The blade landed in the minotaur's back, but the beast ignored him and reached around and jerked it out, never taking his eyes from Shannon.

Cole turned to find Gabriel frantically digging around the blue stone. "Get it," he said and moved to help Shannon.

The minotaur tilted back his head and let out a long, loud roar. Cole used that chance to take Shannon's hand and drag her away from the creature.

"Get away from here," he ordered her, but she didn't move. He looked over his shoulder and found the creature bearing down on them.

He shoved Shannon out of the way and raised his axe. He swung it with all his might and left a gaping wound in the creature's chest, yet the minotaur never slowed as he moved toward Shannon.

Nothing Cole did could get the minotaur to fight him. He saw Shannon stumble to the ground as she backed away, her mouth opened to a silent scream as the minotaur loomed over her.

Cole ran to Gabriel and pushed him out of the way. He raised his war axe and aimed the handle at the stone. Out of the corner of his eye he saw the creature raise his hand to deliver the killing blow to Shannon.

His nightmare was happening before his very eyes. For a moment Cole nearly faltered as he debated on whether to run to Shannon or try and smash the stone. The look of resignation in Shannon's honey brown eyes made his decision.

He sent a silent prayer to the gods and reared back before he slammed the handle of his axe into the blue stone. White light blinded him until he had to cover his eyes with his arm as he fell to his knees. It seemed to last forever, and when he was finally able to open his eyes only the sounds of the night reached him. He looked over and found Shannon huddled in a little ball.

On his hands and knees, Cole moved towards her and took her in his arms. She sobbed into his neck and he rocked her, soothing her.

His gaze caught Gabriel's and they shared a smile.

CHAPTER TWENTY-FIVE

Cole stood beside Gabriel and Shannon as they listened to Aimery. They had won the day, but barely.

"Don't question it," Aimery said as they watched the villagers shifting through their torn village as the sun crested the horizon.

"How are Roderick and Val?" Gabriel asked.

Aimery turned and smiled. "They too have won the day."

Gabriel nodded. "That's good to hear. Where are we off to next?"

Cole heard Shannon's sharp intake of breath as he waited for Aimery's words.

"First, Shannon," Aimery said as he moved to her. "You cannot return to your time. Not now at least."

"I gathered that. Can you tell me anything about the realm I am from?" she said, her voice soft in the morning air.

Aimery shook his head. "Nay, but I can take you someplace where there is another like you."

"Mina," Cole deduced.

"Aye," Aimery said and raised his Fae eyes to him. "Hugh guards Mina and will guard Shannon as well."

Cole clenched his teeth. He didn't want to let her go, but at least he would see her again. If he survived the next mission.

"Who is Hugh?" Shannon asked.

"Leader of the Shields," Cole answered. "He found Mina and decided to stay with her."

"Something interesting happened to Roderick as well," Aimery said as he turned to look at the village.

"What's that?" Gabriel asked.

"He too found his mate."

Cole blinked. "He what?"

Aimery nodded, his fair hair blowing in the wind. "She's a fighter. Saved the day, actually." Aimery turned and stared at Cole. "Don't pass up what has been handed to you."

Cole's mind was filled with questions, but before he could utter one, Aimery called Gabriel to the side, leaving him alone with Shannon.

"Before I leave, there is something I need to tell you," Shannon said as she faced him. "I've never known such fear or had such an adventure as I have with you. Nor have I ever cared for someone like I've come to care for you."

She ducked her head and licked her lips. When she raised her gaze, her honey brown eyes were filled with tears. "I don't expect you to feel the same. I know you are the kind of man who has women falling over him, but I've come to love you. I've come to care about both you and Gabriel. You are my friends now, and I don't want to leave."

"What did you say?" he asked as a slow smile pulled at his lips. He never expected her to return his feelings, and now that she had, he wasn't about to let her go.

"You and Gabriel are my friends."

He chuckled. "I heard that part. I wanted you to repeat the part where you said you loved me. Do you?"

She glanced away and fidgeted with her hands. "I do."

Cole pulled her into his arms and captured her mouth with a kiss he had been longing to give her. She tasted as sweet and fresh as ever, but there was also love and passion mixed in the kiss, making him lightheaded.

He ended the kiss and stared into her beautiful eyes. "I love you, too."

"You do?"

He nodded. "I do, and I'm not about to let you go anywhere without me." He closed his eyes as she wrapped her arms around him and buried her head in his chest.

"I see you two have worked things out," Aimery said as he and Gabriel rejoined them.

Cole nodded. "I have a request."

"I know. I planned to send you with Shannon to Stone Crest. With the gathering of the Chosen, the creatures will begin attacking there."

"What about me?" Gabriel asked.

"You'll meet up with Val. Shall we go?" he asked them.

Cole nodded then moved toward Gabriel. "I'll see

you soon, my brother."

Gabriel clasped forearms with him and nodded. "You will. Be happy." He looked to Shannon and smiled. "Good luck. Until next we meet."

As soon as the words left his mouth he was gone. Cole felt a loss deep within him. Shannon must have understood because she wrapped an arm around his waist and smiled up at him.

"Are you two ready?" Aimery asked.

Cole and Shannon looked into each other's eyes. "Yes," they said in unison.

Aimery sighed deeply as he stared out over *Caer Rhoemyr*, the City of Kings.

They found another of the Chosen. Three of the five were now within the safety of the Fae. But for how long?

How long would the evil wait until they attacked? Only four of the Chosen were needed to end the evil. Hugh, Roderick, and Cole had all found their mates in one of the Chosen. Would Val and Gabriel also be as lucky?

Aimery searched and tried to read the future for the two Shields but saw nothing.

Something was blocking him. Most likely it was the evil.

"There you are," Theron said as he came to stand beside him.

Aimery turned from his balcony to face his king. "I didn't know you were looking for me."

"I wanted to congratulate you and the Shields for finding another of the Chosen. Did Rufina tell me right? Was it indeed Cole?"

Aimery chuckled. "Aye, it was Cole."

"And he also found his mate in her?"

Aimery nodded. "I'm very pleased. He never spoke of it, but I know not remembering where he came from has been a weight upon his shoulders, though he has shouldered it well."

"That he has. He is a good man." Theron turned to Aimery and studied him.

"You took a great interest in him once you found him."

"He was in need." Aimery shifted, growing nervous.

Theron nodded absently. "He was very much in need. Of a father. You filled that role nicely."

Aimery shrugged. "I did what I had to do."

"And treating him like a son? Did you have to do that, as well?"

He tilted his head back and stared at the darkening sky. After a moment, he looked at his king. "He is like a son to me, though I've never admitted that to anyone. Not even Cole."

"Where are Val and Gabriel going?" Theron asked.

Aimery didn't question why his king switched topics. "The Highlands of Scotland. In the year 1436."

"We'll win this, Aimery. The Shields are invincible, and the evil knows it."

Aimery waited until Theron had departed before he turned back to the view of the city. His thoughts were heavy as he thought of Val and Gabriel.

~ ~ ~

Cole laced his hand with Shannon's. "You're going to adore Mina."

"I hope so," she said softly.

Cole smiled and walked to the massive castle gates of Stone Crest. He noticed the castle being repaired from the damage of the gargoyle.

By the time they reached the gates many people were staring at them. He heard a shout and looked toward the castle to see Hugh walking toward them with a bright smile.

Cole embraced his leader. "It's good to see you, Hugh."

"The same here," Hugh said and then looked to Shannon. "Who is this?" His eyes jerked to Cole's as his smile faded. "Have you found another?"

"This is Shannon," he said and pulled her forward to meet Hugh. "Shannon this is Hugh, leader of the Shields."

"Cole? Cole is that you?"

He looked around Hugh to see Mina racing towards them. He grabbed her up in a fierce hug and then set her on her feet.

"I never thought to see you so soon," she said and linked arms with Hugh. "Val and Roderick just left with Elle."

Cole shifted and brought Shannon toward him. "Mina, this is Shannon. Shannon, meet Mina, Hugh's wife and another of the Chosen."

Mina looked from him to Shannon then she let out a whoop and enveloped Shannon in a hug. "All these years I thought I was alone, and then I find two of you in the space of a sennight. Come. Let's go inside and talk."

Cole watched Shannon leave with Mina and sighed.

"I never thought to see that look on your face," Hugh said.

Cole laughed and turned to his leader. "What look?"

"Contentment."

"Love will do that."

"Love?"

Cole nodded. "Aye. Love."

"Well, why didn't you say so?" Hugh said and slapped him on the back. "We need to celebrate!"

Hugh shoved Cole and raced to the castle. Cole laughed for the first time in days as he ran after Hugh. When they rushed into the great hall it was to see Mina and Shannon before the hearth, their heads together as they talked.

Cole swallowed past the lump in his throat. He just saved Shannon from the evil, yet he knew it would come again. Suddenly, Shannon's head lifted, and her gaze turned to him.

Shannon stared into Cole's dark eyes. He looked relaxed and happy, but she saw the worry that tinged his face.

With a smile at Mina, she asked, "Will you excuse me for a moment?"

"Of course," Mina said.

Shannon rose and walked into Cole's open arms. She laid her head on his chest and heard his heart beating in her ear.

"What is it?" she asked.

When he didn't answer, she pulled back and looked into his eyes. "Cole?"

"It's not over."

"I know," she said and took his hands in hers. "But we're one step closer. Three of us have been found. Only one more is needed to end the evil."

He sighed and closed his eyes.

That's when she realized what was really wrong. "You want to be out there fighting."

His eyes opened to show the truth. "It's all I've ever done. It's all I know how to do."

"Not all," she said with a knowing smile.

Cole chuckled and pulled her against him. "My mission is to keep you safe. I willingly do that, but I can't help if I worry over Val and Gabriel."

"We'll always worry," Hugh said as he stepped closer. "We've spent too many years together, and know exactly what we are up against, not to worry."

Mina linked arms with Hugh. "But they have us to help them through that worry."

Shannon tilted her head up and kissed Cole. "You do have me, you know."

His smile was wickedly charming and set her blood on fire. With just a look her breast swelled, her nipples hardened, and her sex ached. "My God, what you do to me."

"I think we need to find a chamber and investigate more."

"Third floor. Fifth chamber on the left," Mina called out as Cole lifted Shannon in his arms and made for the stairs.

Shannon waved to Mina and Hugh before wrapping her arms around Cole. She had found her hero, a man who had not only saved her from certain death, but had saved the world – for the time being.

EPILOGUE

Cole gazed down at Shannon. They had been at Stone Crest for nearly a fortnight with peace and normalcy, something Cole didn't think he would ever see again.

He smoothed the hair from Shannon's face as she stirred and snuggled against him in her sleep. His heart clutched each time he pictured her with the minotaur about to kill her. He saved her once, and he would most likely have to do it many more times before the rest of the Chosen had been found.

Yet, he took what peace they were given and relished it. And each day he was with Shannon he knew more certainly that he couldn't live without her.

"What are you thinking about so seriously this early in the morning?" she asked as she opened her eyes.

He smiled. "You."

"Hmmm. What about me?"

"That I cannot live without you."

She sat up and faced him. "What's really bothering

you?"

"I told you."

She shook her head. "You already have me. You know I return your love, so tell me. What is it really?"

"It isn't enough." As soon as he said the words he realized they were true.

"What else do you want?"

He licked his lips and took her hand in his. "Marry me. I know this realm may end tomorrow or next week, but I want you for my wife. I want to take the sacred vows that bind us to one another."

"You want to marry me?" she asked, her face expressionless.

"More than anything. You've had my heart from the first moment I saw you."

Slowly her face broke into a smile. "You want to marry me?"

"Aye. Will you be my wife?"

"Yes," she screamed and flew into his arms.

They fell backward, and Cole crushed her to him, his lips slanting over hers in a kiss as happiness surrounded him. "Today," he said. "Marry me today."

"Yes. Right after I make love to you," she said and took his cock in her hand.

Read on for a preview of the next SHIELD romance from Donna Grant,
A Forbidden Temptation

CHAPTER ONE

Highlands of Scotland
Winter 1436

The icy fingers of winter had nature firmly in her grasp. The cold slammed into Val's body as soon as stepped through the time portal.

The Highlands, Aimery had told him.

Val blew out a breath and watched it cloud around him though the light of the full moon. He gritted his teeth against the bitter temperatures and gripped his halberd tightly in his hand.

His gaze scanned the darkness, noting the eerie quiet that had descended upon the area. He drew in a deep breath and frowned.

Evil.

Val quickly crouched down in the thick snow. He was out in the open and the nearest grove of trees was several strides away. He would have to make a dash for it, but the heavy blanket of snow could slow him down.

Just as he was about to bolt to the trees, he heard it. The steady flap of wings through the night air. Val raised his head and saw the great beast silhouetted against the dark sky.

"By the gods," he whispered. He hesitated only a heartbeat before he stood and ran to the trees.

The small grove offered little protection. With the shadows hiding him, Val took his time to scout the area. The castle stood high atop one of the smaller mountains with the village below it in the valley. Massive mountains surrounded the area, making it near impossible to reach the town or castle without being seen many leagues away.

His gaze searched the skies again and it didn't take him long to find the creature. With no word from Gabriel, the other Shield, Val would have to do this alone.

He missed having Roderick and Elle with him, but with the great evil closing in quickly, Roderick had to take Elle and watch over her and the other Chosen.

Only one more needed to be found to end the great evil. One more woman who bore the mark of the Chosen and then all this could end.

From the brief conversation he had with Aimery, the Fae Commander had told him that Cole, another Shield, had not only found his mate, but had also found the third Chosen one. It was cause for celebration, but the celebrating would have to wait. Evil still had a tight hold on Earth.

He was about to make his way to the village when he heard the snow crunch. Val tensed and gripped his halberd with both hands, ready to strike at a moment's notice.

Val molded his back to a tree and waited. Out of the corner of his eye, he saw the shadow against the snow. He stepped out and aimed the point of his halberd at the throat of the man.

"Who are you?"

A soft chuckle, devoid of humor reached him. Val tried to peer into the hood of the cloaked form but saw only shadows. The man did not smell of evil, but that didn't mean the man wasn't evil.

"And here I thought I might receive a warm welcome," the man said and swept aside the hood of his cloak.

Val instantly lowered his weapon as he recognized Gabriel. He shook his head and clasped Gabriel's forearm. "I was beginning to wonder where you were."

"I've been scouting the area," Gabriel replied. "I knew Aimery would have you arrive outside the village."

"Did you see it?" Val asked.

Gabriel's silver eyes met his. "I did. I was on my way to the village when you stopped me."

"Then let us go," Val said.

Without another word the two men started toward the village. They had gone only a few steps when they heard the shrill cry.

The men exchanged a look before lengthening their strides to race down the mountain. They saw the flames before they reached the village.

"The creature will be after the Chosen one," Gabriel yelled over the screams of the villagers.

Val nodded. "Let's hope we find her in time."

A DARK GUARDIAN
The first book in the *Shield* series

Dear Reader,

Have you ever wanted to travel through time with weapons crafted by the Fae themselves? To experience adventure so thrilling and dangerous you don't know if you will live to see tomorrow? Now my men and I are faced with fighting creatures only thought to live in legend but which have been brought to Earth by evil bent on annihilating all the realms. That is my life – and I love it.

At least I did until I found myself staring into the angelic, innocent face of Lady Mina of Stone Crest. In all the time I have led the Shields I've trusted my instinct to keep us alive, yet now I don't know what to believe. Everything points to Mina as the evil summoning the creatures, but she proclaims her innocence.

I should be able to see through her lies, if she is indeed lying, but my attraction to her blinds me to even that. The last time I found myself so lured to a woman, it nearly cost me the lives of my men. I cannot allow that to happen again. I *won't* allow that to happen again.

Yet every time she looks at me, begging me with those blue-green eyes to believe her, I find myself sinking further under her spell. Her mouth is a temptation mortal men will never know and her love will either bring me the peace I thought I'd never find – or the death I've managed, thus far, to avoid.

Hugh the Righteous

A KIND OF MAGIC
The second book in the *Shield* series

Greetings Dear Reader,

I was born an immortal prince on the realm of Thales. I lived the life of grandeur, revered and respected, but my one true love was fighting. I was given a special gift in my battle abilities and soon became known as Thales' finest warrior. But all that changed the day my brother died and an evil descended upon my realm. With Thales on the verge of ruin, I bound myself to The Shields to protect the realms from the evil that ravages them. But I have a dark secret that I must atone for. Then and only then can I return to Thales and face my family. My special battle skills and my immortality help to keep my goals in front of me. They have always been clear…

Until Elle.

Elle makes me long for things I cannot have. Her innate goodness makes me want to grasp what she offers with both hands, but I know that we can never have what she seeks. Elle bears a mark that signals her one of a chosen few who were sent to Earth as infants. She and the others who bear the mark must be found and kept hidden from the ancient evil that seeks them, for they hold the key to the evil's ruination.

The only way to keep Elle safe is to keep her by my side, but can I resist the temptation to take her love?

Roderick of Thales

A FORBIDDEN TEMPTATION
The fourth book in the *Shield* series

Salute!

As one of the youngest men ever to have the title of general in ancient Rome's great army, fame and fortune were my bedmates. The Fae chose me for my mastery of any weapon. Though the Shields like to claim they are stronger because of my skills, I know I am only alive today because the Fae found me before my demons could put an end to my life.

Adventure and danger have always ruled my life, and I thrive on the thrill of the hunt. I am loyal to the Shields, willing to give my life to follow Hugh and the others to fulfill their oaths to save the world.

Who would have known following such great men would lead me to Nicole.

She's everything I've ever wanted in a woman and more. She's innocent and pure and beautiful of face and spirit. And she deserves better than me. Yet, every time I think of her in the arms of another I find I cannot let her go.

For better or worse, Nicole has bound herself to me. I just pray that the demons loosen their hold before the past catches up with me and repeats itself.

Valentinus Romulus

A WARRIOR'S HEART
The fifth book in the *Shield* series

Regards Reader,

There are those who would love to rid themselves of painful memories, to forget nasty pasts and mistakes. They say its Hell to live with those memories. I say its Hell to live without them. I have no memories of my past, my friends, or my family.

I owe my life to the Fae who discovered me bleeding and nearly dead at their doorway. They saved me and offered me a new life, regardless of my pat. So I've served the Fae and the Shields since that day. My special knowledge of herbs and healing has been needed to save the Shields countless times. They are my brethren, my family, yet I am alone.

No matter what I search or what questions I ask, I discover nothing to open a doorway in my mind of locked memories. Until I catch a glimpse of a woman who seems as familiar to me as breathing.

Jayna.

Though she claims to not know me, our bodies know each other. I agonize over what she keeps hidden in the depths of her haunted hazel eyes. I fear the dark thoughts that lurk in my heart and wonder at any black deeds in my past. If what I dread comes to pass, death won't come swift enough.

Above all, I must keep Jayna safe. She's the only one what has quieted my soul and shown what serenity was.

Gabriel the Hollow

Thank you for reading **A Dark Seduction**. I hope you enjoyed it! If you liked this book – or any of my other releases – please consider rating the book at the online retailer of your choice. Your ratings and reviews help other readers find new favorites, and of course there is no better or more appreciated support for an author than word of mouth recommendations from happy readers. Thanks again for your interest in my books!

Donna Grant

www.DonnaGrant.com

ABOUT THE AUTHOR

New York Times and *USA Today* bestselling author Donna Grant has been praised for her "totally addictive" and "unique and sensual" stories. She's written more than thirty novels spanning multiple genres of romance including the bestselling Dark King stories, *Dark Craving*, *Night's Awakening*, and *Dawn's Desire* featuring immortal Highlanders who are dark, dangerous, and irresistible. She lives with her husband, two children, a dog, and four cats in Texas.

Connect online at:

www.DonnaGrant.com
www.facebook.com/AuthorDonnaGrant
www.twitter.com/donna_grant
www.goodreads.com/donna_grant/

**Never miss a new book
From Donna Grant!**

Sign up for Donna's email newsletter at
www.DonnaGrant.com

Be the first to get notified of new releases and be eligible for special subscribers-only exclusive content and giveaways. Sign up today!

Made in the USA
Las Vegas, NV
08 March 2021